# Happy Birthday, Dear Amy

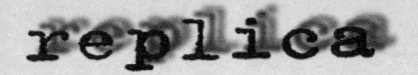

# replica

# Happy Birthday, Dear Amy

## MARILYN KAYE

BANTAM BOOKS
NEW YORK • TORONTO • LONDON • SYDNEY • AUCKLAND

RL 5.5, 008–012
HAPPY BIRTHDAY, DEAR AMY
A Bantam Skylark Book / February 2001

ISBN 0-553-48744-2

**Visit us on the Web! www.randomhouse.com/kids**

Published simultaneously in the United States and Canada

Bantam Skylark is an imprint of Random House Children's Books, a division of Random House, Inc. SKYLARK BOOK and colophon and BANTAM BOOKS and colophon are registered trademarks of Random House, Inc. Bantam Books, 1540 Broadway, New York, New York 10036.

PRINTED IN THE UNITED STATES OF AMERICA

OPM    10    9    8    7    6    5    4    3    2    1

*For my longest-time friend,*
*Roberta Scheer Malickson*

# Happy Birthday, Dear Amy

# one

From her perch on a comfortable lounging chair, Amy Candler basked in the sunshine and gazed out at the shimmering crystal-blue water in the oval swimming pool. This was very clearly *not* the community pool where she and her friends usually congregated. There weren't any screaming kids splashing each other, and no one was jumping up and down on the diving board, yelling like Tarzan. There was no chain-link fence, and no bored teenage lifeguard was ordering people out of the pool. Best of all, Amy didn't have to worry about anyone using the pool as a gigantic toilet.

*This* pool was surrounded by a stone terrace, and the terrace was surrounded by rosebushes. The terrace led to a large, modern house, where there was a bar. Amy knew she could help herself to a soft drink or juice whenever she wanted one, free of charge. From unseen speakers, her favorite radio station played the top ten songs of the week at exactly the right sound level. If she wanted, she could turn it up and not worry about bothering the neighbors. Up here in Beverly Hills, you couldn't even *see* the home of your next-door neighbor.

An uncle of Tasha and Eric Morgan's lived in the house. He had left keys with the Morgans so that they could use the pool while he and his family were on vacation. What Amy couldn't understand was why people who had a house and a pool like this would need to go away for a vacation. But she was certainly glad they had.

"*Summer,*" she murmured blissfully.

"Yeah," Eric sighed.

And Tasha punctuated this with a little moan of pleasure.

Even in Los Angeles, where you could hang out in sunshine practically all year long, there was something special about summer. It wasn't just the weather. Summer meant no school and no homework, and for Amy, it meant her birthday. In fact, her greatest problem at that moment was deciding what kind of cake she wanted for the great event, which was coming up on Saturday. One thing was for sure: It would have to be a big cake.

"Do they make cakes big enough to serve forty people?" she wondered out loud. "Maybe I'll need *two* cakes. Does that mean I have to blow out two sets of candles?"

"Yeah, but you'll get two wishes," Tasha told her.

Eric pretended to groan. "Do we have to sing 'Happy Birthday to You' twice?"

Amy giggled in delight. She'd never had such a big birthday party before. But then, she'd never turned thirteen before. *Thirteen.* The beginning of her real teen years.

"Do you feel any different now that you're thirteen?" she asked Tasha. Her friend had celebrated her birthday two months earlier.

"I'm not sure," Tasha said. "Most of the time I think I'm exactly the same as I was when I was twelve. It's not like I *look* any different. But sometimes I think I *feel* a little different. More mature."

"That's just in your head," Eric said.

Tasha looked at him scornfully. "That's where mature feelings *are,* Eric. In your head."

"Yeah, in *my* head," Eric chortled. "Not yours. I can guarantee, you are absolutely no more mature now than you were two months ago."

"Okay, you guys, cut it out," Amy said mildly. She was accustomed to hearing the brother and sister tease each other. As an only child, sometimes she even envied them. "Eric, did you feel any different on your thirteenth birthday?"

"That was two years ago," Eric replied. "I don't remember. I don't *think* so. I mean, it's not like anything changes overnight."

Amy yawned and stretched lazily. She thought *she* was beginning to change a little. Nothing major. She was just dimly aware of an achy sensation in her arms and legs. She wasn't worried, though. After all, she was going through puberty, and according to all the articles in all the teen magazines she read, these were perfectly normal growing pains.

Except that Amy wasn't a perfectly normal girl. She certainly wasn't like any ordinary twelve-year-old on the verge of turning thirteen. For one thing, she hadn't been born thirteen years ago. In fact, she hadn't been *born* at all—she'd been genetically engineered. Along with thirteen others, she'd been designed and created from carefully selected cell samples and had developed inside a series of test tubes and under microscopes.

She, along with the others, had grown from fetus to infant inside an incubator. What she called her birthday was the day that Nancy Candler, scientist and junior member of Project Crescent, rescued the last remaining experimental unit from the burning lab. The scientists had intentionally triggered the explosion after learning that the government agency funding the project wanted to create a master race using the clones. Nancy and the others felt this was unethical. So they set fire to the lab to make the agents believe that the clones had all perished. In reality, the clones had been whisked away and sent to live with adoptive families around the world. Nancy had taken the infant clone Amy, Number Seven, home to raise as her own daughter.

Ordinary aches and pains weren't a common experience for Amy. Her genes had been manipulated and treated so that she would develop a perfect physique. She was always healthy.

"Are there really going to be forty people at your party?" Tasha asked. "Did everyone accept their invitations?"

"Everyone," Amy confirmed. "Even Linda Riviera."

"How come you invited *her*?" Eric wanted to know. "You don't even like her. I don't like her."

"I had to invite Linda because I invited Simone Cusack, and Simone is Linda's best friend now. And I had to invite Simone because she invited me to *her* birthday party. Don't worry, there are going to be so many people there, you won't even have to see Linda."

Amy was confident of that. This was going to be a real bash, a mix of boys and girls from the seventh, eighth, and ninth grades at Parkside Middle School. They were gathering at the home of Dr. David Hopkins, a friend of Amy and her mother's, who had kindly donated his beach house for the party. There would be beach volleyball, a cookout, and dancing on the patio.

"Have you decided what you're going to wear?" Amy asked Tasha.

"My pink crop top and black jeans."

"Perfect," Amy said.

"What about you?" Tasha asked. "Did you get something new?"

Amy nodded. "It'll be a surprise." She couldn't help smiling as she thought about the crisp white halter sundress, still covered in the plastic from the shop and hanging in her closet. It was so cool, and it fit perfectly.

"I've got a surprise too," Eric announced.

Amy's eyes narrowed suspiciously. "This isn't a costume party, Eric."

"It's not that kind of surprise," he assured her. "I think you'll like it." He was looking very confident and very pleased with himself, and Amy just hoped that the surprise wasn't going to be anything too embarrassing. Not that Eric would ever try to embarrass her on purpose. He wouldn't do anything to spoil her party.

And there wouldn't be any letdown after the great event. The very next day, she was leaving with her mother and Dr. Dave for the Grand Canyon, where they would spend ten days hiking and camping.

Eric and Tasha, too, were heading out of L.A. a couple of days after her party. At that very moment, Eric was reading about their destination from a pamphlet titled "Welcome to Camp Riverbend."

"Hey, Tasha, it says here there's a weekly dance for campers over the age of twelve from both camps. If you give me some money, I'll bribe another counselor to dance with you."

"No thanks," Tasha retorted. "And don't forget, Eric, you're just a *junior* counselor, not a *real* one."

Eric was ready with a comeback. "Better to be a junior counselor than an ordinary camper."

"Stop it, Eric," Amy said automatically. She knew very well that Tasha wasn't thrilled at the prospect of going off to summer camp. She turned to Tasha with a sympathetic expression. "Are you absolutely, positively sure you can't get out of this?"

"I've tried," Tasha told her. "But my parents are being really obnoxious. My mother says she doesn't want me hanging around doing nothing, and my father thinks I need more exercise." She tried to sound casually annoyed, but there was a slight tremor in her voice and Amy knew why. They'd talked about this many times before. Tasha was worried that all the other girls at the camp would be athletic types, which she definitely wasn't. She was afraid she'd feel out of place at Camp Riverbend and that the others would make fun of her. Having her brother across the lake at the boys' camp wasn't any comfort to her.

Personally, Amy thought it was mean of Tasha's parents to make her go. It was awful the way parents tried to run kids' lives sometimes. And the kids couldn't really fight back. Amy's own mother used to give her a lot of unwanted advice, but lately she'd been letting Amy make more of her own decisions, and Amy was glad of that.

Lying there in the warm sun, contemplating a dip in the cool water, she marveled at how lucky she was. She had a super boyfriend and a wonderful best friend. Her mother was reasonably cool, for a mother. Amy had a birthday party and a camping trip and a whole summer of fun to look forward to. Yes, she was definitely a lucky girl, and good feelings washed over her.

There was no way she could know that in just a few days, she would be in a very different state of mind.

# two

It had been a long time since Amy had had *that* dream. Almost a year, in fact. In the recurring dream, she was trapped in a glass container while fire raged around her. She could feel the heat from the flames, and she was frightened. Then the container was opened and she was lifted out and carried away from the danger.

She had been having this dream for as long as she could remember. A year earlier, she'd learned its meaning. The dream was a recollection of the day Nancy Candler had rescued her.

Her mother and the other scientists had discovered

that the organization behind Project Crescent was trying to create a master race of superhuman clones through whom they would control the world. Being good, ethical people, the scientists could not allow this to happen. So they sent the thirteen infant Amys away and destroyed all evidence that the clones had ever been created. Amy, Number Seven, was the last clone to be removed from the laboratory as it went up in flames.

Once Amy understood the dream, once she knew who and what she was, the dream came to her less frequently. She had it only once in a while, at times of crisis or when she was really bothered by something. Maybe her thirteenth birthday was an even more important, bigger deal than she thought it was, because the night before, she had the dream again.

When she opened her eyes and saw the familiar ceiling of her own bedroom, she experienced the same relief she used to feel when she realized she'd been dreaming. But as she lay there, still groggy, she experienced something else, too. Something different . . . a physical sensation in her arms and legs . . . and in her hands and feet as well. Even in her head. In fact, all over her body.

It was a strange sensation, not a pain exactly or even an ache. It wasn't a *bad* feeling. It was just a *feeling*, and she couldn't identify it or come up with a word to describe it. Growing pains, she thought sleepily.

She still wasn't fully awake, and she considered closing her eyes and going back to sleep, but decided against it. This was her birthday, her once-a-year special day, and she couldn't waste it sleeping. With some effort, she swung her legs over the side of the bed.

Her feet hit the floor with a thud that was peculiar. Standing up was strange too—it seemed to take her a second longer than usual to get herself into an upright position. Once she was standing, she experienced an odd dizziness. Gazing around the room, she could see that nothing had changed; all her stuff was there, and everything was where it was supposed to be. And yet it wasn't *right*. It was like she was seeing her room from a different perspective.

I'm still sleeping, she thought. This is a dream. Walking unsteadily, with a sense of heaviness, she made her way around the bed to her closet, where a full-length mirror hung on the inside of the door.

Yes, she was definitely dreaming. Once she'd opened the closet door and looked into the mirror, she was certain of it. Because the reflection in the glass wasn't hers.

Amy was gazing at an adult, a woman who looked as if she was in her twenties. Her hair was brown, similar in color to Amy's hair. In fact, her hair was *exactly* the same color, and she wore it in the same shoulder-length style. The woman stared back at Amy through eyes that were the same shade of brown.

Amy blinked. At the same time, the woman in the mirror blinked.

Then Amy heard her bedroom door open. A voice started singing "Happy Birthday to You." She turned to see her mother coming in, carrying a plate that held a muffin—blueberry, Amy presumed. That was her favorite and the kind her mother brought her every year on her birthday. Sticking out of the muffin was a lit candle. Nancy Candler had cupped a hand around the tiny flame to keep it from going out. She sang softly, smiling, but when she looked up—she screamed.

The plate, the muffin, and the candle fell to the floor. Automatically, Amy's eyes dropped to the things on the carpet. The fall had blown out the flame, so there was no danger of fire. Turning back to the mirror, she saw that the woman there looked just as surprised as *she* felt. And behind her, Nancy was still screaming.

Suddenly Amy realized she wasn't dreaming. She was wide awake, living and breathing, on the morning of her thirteenth birthday. And that grown-up woman in the mirror—that was *her*.

She didn't have long to absorb this revelation. Suddenly her mother was standing before her, shaking her violently.

"Who are you? What have you done with my daughter?"

Amy could easily have pushed her mother away, but she didn't move. She was too stunned to do anything but stand there, limp and dazed, and allow herself to be shaken.

"Where is she? Where is Amy?" Nancy shrieked.

Finally Amy found her voice. But the words sounded different, deeper, and not at all like herself.

"Mom . . . Mom, it's me. I'm Amy."

# three

Through an open window in the guest bedroom on the second floor of Dr. Dave's beach house, Amy could see baby-blue skies, turquoise water, and a beach composed of sand in various shades of white, beige, and light brown. She could hear the seagulls, even the ones way off in the distance that were just a spot on the horizon, and she could smell the salt in the ocean waves that lapped on the shore. Her senses didn't seem to have changed at all. Only her size, her shape . . . her face, her body, and everything else.

She tightened the belt that was holding up a pair of her mother's jeans and eavesdropped on the conversation between her mother and Dr. Dave, on the other side of the bedroom door.

"I've examined her," Dr. Dave was saying. "From what I can see, there's nothing physically wrong with her. Her pulse and blood pressure are right where they should be, she doesn't have a fever, her reflexes are fine, and her heart sounds are normal. She's a perfectly healthy young woman, around twenty-five years old."

His words did nothing to ease the concern in Nancy's voice. "But she's *not* a twenty-five-year-old woman, Dave! She's a thirteen-year-old girl! What happened?"

"It looks as if something triggered her cells to move into fast-forward," Dr. Dave said. "She's aged at least twelve years overnight. And I think I know why."

As Amy listened to his explanation, she thought his theory was right. According to Dr. Dave, at an early stage in Project Crescent there had been some discussion about implanting a genetic code that would accelerate cellular growth in the clones. That way, the scientists would be able to determine very quickly whether or not the experiment was successful.

"This was before you joined the team," Dr. Dave told Amy's mother. "Dr. Jaleski vetoed the idea. He said it would be unethical to deprive the clones of experiencing a normal infancy, and that it could have serious repercussions on their quality of life."

"Did everyone agree with him?" Nancy wanted to know.

There was a slight hesitation before Dr. Dave replied. "Almost everyone."

Amy could imagine her mother's eyes darkening. "Grace Atkinson. She knew about the organization that was supporting the project," Nancy said. "I bet she didn't care if the clones had any quality of life. She probably disregarded Dr. J's decision and put the implants into the clones."

"We don't know this for sure," Dr. Dave cautioned her. "She may not have interfered with all the clones. She might simply have selected Number Seven at random. I could call Grace, but she'd only deny it."

Amy had met Dr. Atkinson, and what Dr. Dave said made sense. The woman was all science, no heart.

"What about Amy?" Nancy asked, and Amy could hear the tremor in her voice. "What's going to happen to her? Will she continue to age?"

"I can't be sure, but I don't think so," the doctor replied. "The original idea behind the implants was to bring them rapidly to a mature adult stage physically and then allow them to age naturally."

"Can she be brought back to her real age?"

"Theoretically, yes. If the implant can be located and removed, or if the genetic code can be reversed, she

**17**

should automatically return to her normal physiological level. But this would require testing and equipment that I don't have here at home. We need to get her into a hospital."

"Then let's take her to one, right now, and have that implant removed," Nancy said.

"It's not that easy," Dr. Dave said. "She'll need a whole series of tests just to locate the device. All the tests, and any possible operation, will have to be performed secretly. We can't risk alerting people, even hospital staff, to Amy's situation. Remember, Nancy, if Grace is behind this, then the organization knows that something should be happening to Amy right about now. They'll be looking for a special girl who's aged twelve years overnight."

"So what do we do?"

"She doesn't appear to be in any immediate danger from her condition," Dr. Dave said. "We have a suite at my hospital that's unknown to the public and most of the staff. Movie stars use it when they come in for cosmetic surgery. Let me see if I can arrange for Amy to be admitted there."

As he continued to talk about hospital plans, Amy wandered over to a chest of drawers. A mirror hung over it. It would provide her with a view of only her head and shoulders, but that was the best she could do in this room. The immediate shock of the morning had passed, and she examined herself closely.

It was such a strange sensation, looking at herself as a stranger. Now that she knew who she was looking at, she could recognize herself—but she doubted anyone else would be able to. It was as if she'd asked a fortune-teller to reveal what she'd look like as an adult, and she was now gazing into a crystal ball. She supposed most kids would love to know what they were going to look like in the future.

But this wasn't the future. This was *now*, Amy Candler's thirteenth birthday. She was supposed to be entering her teenage years today. Instead, it seemed that she had completely skipped them. Her teen years were in a past that had never happened. She'd lost them forever. It wasn't fair!

She took a deep breath to steady her nerves and tried to look at the woman in the mirror objectively. Was she pretty? Yes . . . not a supermodel or Miss Universe, but not bad. Her complexion was nice, with a peachy tone and no zits. Her hair seemed to be a little thicker, even a shade lighter. Her eyes looked larger. But it was in the shape of her face that she could see a big difference . . . it was narrow now, with higher cheekbones. Her nose was different too, longer, and it didn't turn up at the end anymore. Her ears were a little bigger, but not *too* big.

She smiled, opening her mouth. Her teeth were very white and straight. She turned her face from side to side. If she held her head at a certain angle, so that the sun shone on her hair, she was almost blond, and she thought she looked a little bit like Rachel on *Friends*.

Gathering the hair in her hands, she pulled it back away from her face and decided she looked almost elegant. She envisioned big gold earrings. And makeup, lots of makeup. Glitter eye shadow, black eyeliner, mascara, red lipstick. Her mother couldn't make a fuss about that. A woman in her twenties had the right to wear as much makeup as she wanted to.

So her face was okay. What about the rest of her? Impulsively she climbed onto the bed to get a better look.

It was amazing, what twelve years could do to a girl's figure. She gazed at her body in awe. It had really filled out. She wouldn't call herself fat, but she wasn't skinny, either. There were curves where none had existed before. As for her chest . . . visions of halters and bandeaus and tube tops filled her mind. She could hold tops like that up now. She put her hands on her hips and twisted first one way, then the other. Maybe being an adult wasn't so awful. . . .

"Amy, what are you doing?"

Clearly, Amy's having become an adult wasn't having any effect on the way her mother spoke to her. Amy hopped off the bed guiltily.

"Sorry, Mom. I was just trying to get a better look at myself."

Her mother winced, and Amy thought how strange it must be for her, hearing her daughter's voice coming from the mouth of an adult stranger. Or *was* it her voice? Listening to herself, it was hard to tell.

"Mom, do I still sound like me? Is my voice the same?"

"It's a little deeper," Nancy said. She sat down on the bed. "Honey, I want you to know, everything's going to be all right. Dr. Hopkins and I are going to do everything possible to—to—"

"I know," Amy broke in. "I heard you talking. Do I really have to go into a hospital?"

"It's the only way, honey. But I think—" Once again Nancy was interrupted, this time by the sound of the doorbell downstairs. "Who could that be?"

"Probably Tasha and Eric," Amy said. "They were supposed to come early and help me decorate."

Her mother's face was a complete blank. She'd forgotten all about the party. Amy supposed she really couldn't blame her. What had happened that morning would drive everything else out of anyone's mind. Except Amy's.

"My party, Mom. My birthday party. Remember?"

To her mother's credit, Nancy was very upset. "Ohmigod. Oh, Amy. Honey, I'm so sorry."

There was a rap on the door, and Dr. Dave stuck his head in. "Tasha and Eric are here," he announced. "They're outside on the terrace. I don't know what to tell them."

"The truth!" Amy suggested. "They know all about me."

But Dr. Dave didn't agree. "Amy, until we understand what's happened to you, I think we'd better keep this . . . this situation . . . a secret."

"Tasha and Eric can keep secrets," Amy protested, but her mother agreed with Dr. Dave.

"The fewer people who know, the better," she said. "The shock of seeing you like this—well, even your closest friends might not be able to deal with it."

There was no point in arguing. Amy could see that her mother was adamant. "But what about my party?" Even as she asked, she feared she already knew the answer.

"It's too late to cancel," her mother said. She turned to Dr. Hopkins. "What do you think? We have to tell them something."

A few moments later, lying on the bed and staring miserably at the ceiling, Amy listened through the open window as her mother told her friends the story that had been hastily concocted.

"She woke up with a terrible pain in her side," Nancy explained. "I rushed her to the hospital. It turned out to be her appendix. It was terribly infected."

"Fortunately, I was there to do the appendectomy," Dr. Dave said. "She's resting comfortably in a private recovery room now."

Amy wished she could get a look at her friends' reactions. At least she could hear them respond. Tasha was clearly frightened. "Is she going to be okay?"

"Oh, yes, she'll be fine," Nancy assured her. "She's very weak right now, but she'll recover."

Eric sounded more skeptical. "I don't get it. Amy's supposed to be perfect. How could her appendix get infected?"

Dr. Dave answered him. "We can't be sure. We don't know everything about Amy."

"But you must have an idea why this happened," Eric said. "You're a doctor, you helped make her!"

The doctor tried to come up with a plausible diagnosis. "Well, you know that as an organ, the appendix is essentially useless. Maybe Amy's body recognized this and rejected the organ."

"But why *now*?" Eric persisted. "Why didn't her body reject her appendix a long time ago?"

Dr. Dave was getting impatient. "Eric, I don't *know*. Believe me, as soon as I figure it all out, I'll tell you."

Amy had a feeling Eric wouldn't be satisfied with that. She knew *she* wouldn't be. It took every ounce of willpower to keep herself from sticking her head out the window and letting Eric see what had happened to her. Why couldn't her mother trust Amy's friends like *she* did? Why was it that adults never had any faith in kids?

Right now, her mother was rattling off the rest of the story they'd invented. "Amy wants her birthday celebration to go on, even though she can't be here. I'm going to videotape the party so she can watch it tomorrow while she recovers in the hospital."

"We could come to the hospital and watch it with her," Tasha suggested.

Nancy was vague. "Well, we'll see how she's feeling."

And so Amy Candler's thirteenth birthday party, the event she'd been looking forward to for so long, went on just as it had been planned—only without the birthday girl. But from the window seat, Amy had a panoramic view of the festivities.

There they were, forty friends and classmates, cavorting on the beach, playing volleyball, building sand castles, having a great time. She could hear them laughing. Were any of them even *thinking* about her? She could see Simone Cusack and Linda Riviera, strutting around in bikinis that Amy thought were way too mature for them. To wear a skimpy suit like that, you needed a body like, like—like what Amy had now. She envisioned herself walking onto the beach in one of those bikinis. Eric's eyes would pop out. Thinking of eyes made her realize her own eyes were itchy, and she rubbed them.

Now Dr. Dave was holding the video camera and taping Nancy as she brought the cake outside. Everyone was singing "Happy Birthday to You." After that, Tasha suggested that the whole group blow out the candles and make a collective wish—that Amy would get better fast. Amy could still feel the itch in her eyes, only now it was more of a burning sensation.

Then there was a sound overhead from a low-flying plane. Eric pointed it out to everyone. "That's my surprise," he said, and Dr. Dave focused the camera on it. The plane dragged a banner across the sky, and the red letters stood out against the pale blue.

HAPPY BIRTHDAY AMY, the banner declared. Amy could hear the crowd oohing and aahing.

Now she knew what that burning feeling in her eyes meant. If there had ever been a time in her life when she was entitled to feel sorry for herself, this was it. She broke down and cried.

# four

From his own bedroom window, Eric couldn't see Amy's house next door. He was facing the wrong direction. But he knew there was a view from his sister's room.

Tasha's door was open, and the room was empty. He went in and opened the window. If he stuck his head way out and leaned to the right, he could see one of Amy's bedroom windows. He stared long and hard, but he couldn't detect any movement inside the room.

"What are you doing here?" Tasha demanded.

It was pretty obvious, but Eric answered her anyway. "Looking out your window." He pulled his head back in.

"Why? You've got windows." She crossed the room and joined him. "And you shouldn't open it anyway—the air-conditioning's on." As she closed the window, she looked out to the right. "You were trying to see into Amy's bedroom," she accused him. "She's not there, Eric. She's still in the hospital."

"Yeah, that's what everyone *says*," Eric muttered.

"You think they're lying?" Tasha asked in disbelief.

"Well, *something* weird is going on!" he declared. "Why can't we go visit her at the hospital? We can't even call her!" He stared out at the front door of the house, which he could see clearly. It was opening. "I'm going to talk to Ms. Candler," he announced abruptly.

"Eric, don't bother Amy's mother!" Tasha called after him, but Eric had already raced down the stairs.

As he ran out of the house, he called out, "Ms. Candler!"

Nancy was heading toward her car, but she paused and waited for Eric to catch up. As he approached, she smiled, but it looked like she was having to work hard at keeping the smile on her face.

"Hello, Eric. I thought you would have left for camp by now."

"Tomorrow," he said. "At least, that's when I'm supposed to leave. But now I'm thinking maybe I shouldn't go."

"Why not?"

"Because of Amy. I'm worried about her, so I might stick around till I know she's okay."

Nancy's smile was starting to slip. "There's no need for that, Eric. Amy's going to be all right."

"Then why is she still in the hospital? A friend of mine had his appendix out, and he was home in two days."

"Dr. Hopkins wants to make sure the infection hasn't affected any other organs. But there's nothing for you to worry about, I assure you. She's coming along just fine."

"Then I want to see her," he said. "Today, before I leave."

Nancy shook her head. "No, she can't have any visitors—I told you that yesterday. She's in isolation."

"Is that normal?" Eric asked. "Why does she have to be isolated?"

"Amy's not normal, Eric, you know that. The doctor just wants to take every possible precaution. No visitors, that's the rule."

"Why can't I talk to her on the phone?" he asked.

Nancy Candler was beginning to look seriously annoyed. "You can't call Amy because she doesn't have a phone in her room. I won't let her have a phone because I know all her friends would call, and I don't want her to wear herself out talking. She needs to rest. This is for her own good, Eric. I wish you'd try to appreciate that."

Eric gazed at her steadily. There was absolutely nothing in her words, in her voice, or in her expression that suggested she wasn't telling the truth. There was no reason why he shouldn't believe her.

And yet he didn't.

"Excuse me, Eric, I have to go. I'll tell Amy you asked about her."

He watched her get into the car, back out of the driveway, and take off. Long after she'd disappeared, he was still staring in that direction, trying to decide what to do.

At dinner that evening, his mother asked him and Tasha if they'd finished packing for camp. Tasha nodded morosely. "But I could unpack in five seconds if you'd let me out of this," she said.

"Now, Tasha, I felt the same way when I was your age," her mother told her. "And I loved my camp experience. I'd be very surprised if you don't feel the same way."

"Prepare to be surprised," Tasha muttered.

"Eric, are you all packed?" Mrs. Morgan asked.

That was when Eric made his announcement. "I'm not going."

Both his parents and his sister stared at him. His father was the first to find his voice. "Now *you* don't want to go to camp?"

"I want to know what's going on with Amy."

His mother was bewildered. "Amy had her appendix out, that's all. Nancy says she's coming along just fine."

"Yeah, well, I want to see for myself," Eric stated. "I'm not leaving till I've seen her."

"Did you ask her mother?" Tasha wanted to know.

Eric nodded. "She says Amy can't have any visitors and she can't have phone calls, either."

"But she's still doing okay, right?" Tasha asked anxiously.

"That's what her mother told me," Eric said.

"Then that's that," Mrs. Morgan said briskly. "You'll go to camp tomorrow, and Amy will recover, and you'll see her when you get back in three weeks."

Eric shook his head stubbornly. "I'm not leaving town till I've seen her."

"You're being ridiculous," Mr. Morgan said sharply. "You wanted this counseling job, and you were lucky enough to get it. The camp is counting on you to be there. You can't back out now."

"I don't want to back out!" Eric declared. "I just want to see Amy. If I can see her tonight, I'll go to camp tomorrow."

His father's face was getting red. "If Nancy Candler says Amy can't have visitors, then you can't see her."

"Then I won't go to camp," Eric said.

His mother was aghast. "Eric, do you realize how irresponsible you're being? You signed a contract with the camp!"

Tasha looked up hopefully. "If Eric doesn't go to camp, do I still have to go?"

"Eric's going to camp!" Mr. Morgan thundered.

Eric shoved his chair back from the table and stood up. "I'm going to my room." As he stomped out of the dining room, his mother called after him.

"Make sure you pack a warm sweater, Eric—it can get cold at night in the country."

He couldn't believe it. It was like the argument hadn't even taken place. They didn't take him seriously; they were treating him like he was a little kid. Slamming the door to his room, he threw himself on his bed. He felt like he was about to explode, and he wanted to talk to someone about this. He wanted to talk to Amy.

But Amy wasn't available. And no one else seemed to be terribly concerned about it.

# f 5 ve

It really wasn't so bad for a hospital room. The walls were pale yellow instead of stark white, the bedsheets were pale blue, and yellow and blue flowered curtains covered the window. An alcove held a little sofa and an armchair. It didn't look sterile or antiseptic, like most hospital rooms. In fact, it looked more like a hotel suite.

But despite the cheerful decoration, it was still a hospital room. And as far as Amy was concerned, it might as well have been a jail cell.

Lying on the bed, she aimed the remote at the TV that was suspended from the ceiling and hit buttons at random. Images flickered across the screen, but nothing grabbed her interest. She picked up the remote that operated her bed and played with that, raising her knees and lowering them. Then her feet, then her head . . . that wasn't very amusing either.

She listened to make sure no one was out in the hall and coming toward the room. Then she got out of bed. Dragging the machine that was monitoring her heart rate, she went to the window. There wasn't much to see from there—she was too high up, and smog covered the city. Even super-vision couldn't penetrate the thick gray stuff.

Leaving the window, she went into the bathroom and looked in the mirror. Would she ever get used to this face? she wondered. She'd been looking like this for three days now, but she still felt a little shiver every time she saw her reflection. She studied her face for a moment. She wanted to ask her mother to bring her a cosmetics kit so that she could experiment with her new adult features.

But what was the point of putting on makeup when no one would be seeing her? She wasn't allowed to have any visitors, except for her mother. There was Dr. Dave, of course, but he acted more like a doctor than a friend. He was putting her through a zillion tests, trying to figure out what had happened to her body and how she could be changed back to her normal self.

A couple of nurses came in now and then, smiling professionally and saying things like "How are we feeling today?", but clearly they'd been told not to speak personally to her. The same was true for the people who brought her meals and changed her bed linens. They glanced at her curiously, murmured greetings, and scurried out as soon as they were finished with whatever they'd come in to do. They probably thought she was somebody famous in hiding, like a movie star having a face-lift, and they couldn't understand why she looked so unfamiliar.

Amy understood why her situation had to be kept a secret. She knew the dangers of being discovered, especially by the organization. But that didn't make being here any easier. She was bored, and she was lonely.

She heard the door to the room open, and then Dr. Dave's anxious voice. "Amy? Amy?"

Shuffling out of the bathroom, she said, "Here I am."

"What are you doing out of bed?" Dr. Dave asked. "I told you I wanted you to stay as still as possible today, so I could get an accurate reading from your heart monitor."

"I had to use the bathroom," she muttered. "Sorry." She got back into bed. "What's happening today?"

"We need to draw some more blood," he said. "And we'll take new X rays. I'm going to schedule a bone scan, an MRI, an EEG . . ." He rattled off more initials, and Amy lost interest. It would be another day just like the day before. She'd be lying there while people did things to her.

Like right now. The doctor was bent over her, feeling her neck. "Does this hurt?"

"No," she replied.

He pressed other areas of her neck. "Here? Can you feel this? What about here, does this hurt?"

"No, no, and no," Amy replied. "I feel fine. I'm not tired or anything. In fact, I've got a lot of energy."

"Mmm." He wasn't even listening to her. He went to the foot of her bed and looked at her chart. He made a notation, but she was sure it had nothing to do with what she'd just said.

"When can I get out of here?" she asked.

He was still studying her chart. When he finally looked up, he smiled. But his next comment made it clear that he hadn't heard her question. "How about something special for lunch? I know what hospital food is like. I could stop by McDonald's and bring something back for you."

Amy stared back at him without smiling. Did he

really think a Big Mac would improve her mood? Maybe he thought a Happy Meal could make her happy. That was how she was being treated—like a little kid who only needed french fries to cheer her up. "No, thanks."

After he'd left, Amy lay there, feeling lonelier than before he'd come in. This was so stupid! Eric and Tasha were leaving for camp that afternoon, and she wasn't even allowed to say goodbye to them. Would it really be so awful to call them? The sound of her voice wouldn't tell them what she looked like.

She slipped out of bed and looked in her purse. There was plenty of change lying on the bottom. She scooped it up and dragged the heart monitor to the door. Opening it, she looked up and down the hall. There had to be a pay phone around somewhere.

A woman in a white coat materialized. "Is anything wrong? Do you need something, dear?"

"Can I make a phone call?"

She might as well have asked if she could perform a little brain surgery in her spare time. Kindly but firmly, the woman sent her back to bed.

Lunch came, and Amy ate it without even noticing what it was. Then she flipped through some magazines her mother had left for her the day before: a Delia's catalog, *Seventeen*, *YM*. But she couldn't feel any real interest in the fashions she saw. These were clothes that would look good on a thirteen-year-old, she thought. Not on a young woman of twenty-five. She would ask her mother to bring her *Vogue* and *In Style*.

Nancy Candler arrived later that afternoon. By that time, Amy was ready to climb the walls.

"Fine! I'm fine! And I want to get out of here!" Amy practically screamed when her mother asked her how she was feeling.

"Sweetie, you know you have to stay in the hospital. This is the only place where we can figure out how to help you."

Amy fell back on her pillow. "I'm *b-o-o-o-r-ed!*" she wailed.

"How about if I bring in a VCR?" her mother offered. "And some movies? You could watch the video of your party."

"How thrilling," Amy said, and she made no effort to hide her sarcasm. "How about some R-rated movies? I'm over eighteen now."

"Mmm." Now her mother was looking at her medical chart, not listening to a word Amy was saying. Amy watched her mother's face as she flipped through the chart's pages.

"Anything interesting?"

Nancy looked up, and her face bore the same artificially bright smile Dr. Dave had been wearing. "Nothing for you to worry about." She went back to reading the chart.

Amy frowned. It was *her* body. She was entitled to worry about it if she wanted to. And she was definitely entitled to know what was going on with it. "Mom, I've been thinking. Maybe I'm going to stay this way, and I just have to deal with it."

"Mmm . . ."

"I have to think about what I'm going to do. I can't go back to middle school. Maybe I could take a high school equivalency test and apply to a university. Somewhere out of town, where no one knows me. I'd be older than most of the other freshmen, but I probably wouldn't stand out too much. And then I could—"

Her mother interrupted. "Have you been having any headaches?"

"No! Mom, did you hear what I was saying?"

Her mother's blank expression was answer enough.

"Mom, if I don't get back to the way I was—"

Again her mother didn't let her finish. "Oh, sweetie, don't worry about that. We've just begun searching for the cause. I know this is a nightmare for you, but I promise you, we'll find the answer."

*When?* Amy wanted to ask, but she knew her mother couldn't answer that. And it wouldn't have been a nightmare if she hadn't been stuck in this place.

"Do you want anything?" her mother asked. "Ice cream? How about a pizza?"

Amy grimaced. Why was everyone trying to cheer her up with food?

Dr. Dave came in. "Hi, Nancy. Here, I just got some new lab results. Take a look."

"Can I see them?" Amy asked.

Neither of them replied. Their heads were bent together as they studied the papers. "Interesting," Nancy murmured.

"What's interesting?" Amy asked.

"You can see that the ratio hasn't changed," the doctor pointed out.

Nancy nodded. "It's still within normal range."

Amy tried again. "What's within normal range?"

"What are you checking today?" Nancy asked Dr. Dave. "Serum cholesterol?"

He nodded. "And I'll run a glucose tolerance. Not that I expect it to tell us much, but her blood sugar could be an issue."

Amy's frustration had reached new heights. "What are you talking about?" she demanded. Her voice was shrill.

Her mother actually looked up. "You wouldn't under-stand, sweetie, and it's nothing for you to worry about. Everything's going to be fine." She lowered her voice and continued to talk to Dr. Dave. They spoke in a litany of meaningless letters and numbers, and they used a lot of words that Amy didn't understand. But she could pick up enough to realize that she wasn't in any im-mediate danger and all her body parts seemed to be working as well as they ever had. She was not a sick person.

Amy held her temper until Dr. Dave left. Then, alone with her mother, she exploded. "This is crazy! I don't want to lie around in the hospital like I've got a disease! I feel fine. There's nothing wrong with me— I'm just older, that's all!"

Her mother was taken aback by the outburst. "Sweetie, honey, I know this is scary for you. I know how frightened you must be, but you must be brave and—"

"I'm not frightened, I'm *mad*!" Amy broke in. "You and Dr. Dave, you're not telling me anything, you're not even asking my opinion! Maybe—maybe I don't want to be cured. Maybe I'm happy like this. If all my body parts are working and nothing's wrong with me, maybe I should just stay this way! Can't I have some say in this?"

"Don't be silly," her mother said. "You're upset. You don't know what you're saying."

"Stop treating me like a child!"

Nancy sighed deeply. "Amy, you *are* a child, even if you look like an adult. And you can't make your own decisions about your treatment. We're all doing the best we can, but you'd just better get used to the fact that you might be here for a while."

"How long?"

"Amy, I don't know! As long as it takes!"

Which could be weeks, Amy thought. Or months, even. She could be spending the entire summer here in the hospital. Or maybe the rest of her life.

The possibilities were overwhelming, too awful to even contemplate. But one look at her mother's face told her there was no point in continuing to argue. According to her mother, she wouldn't be getting out of this place anytime soon.

Unless . . .

She fell silent and tried to think. She responded to her mother's efforts to start a conversation with little more than a yes or a no or a shrug of her shoulders. Long after her mother had given up and left for the evening, she was still thinking, hard.

Her mother would be upset, there was no doubt in

Amy's mind about that. But Amy didn't feel she had any choice.

She watched the clock. The nurses would be changing shifts at eleven. They'd be busy, exchanging information, and that might be a good time to put her plan into action. It was now ten-thirty. Carefully she removed the tapes that attached the heart monitor to her chest. Then she slipped out of bed and got dressed.

At precisely one minute before eleven, she opened her door a crack and peered out. As she expected, the staff was meeting in the little room behind the nurses' station. She could see them through a window, which meant they could also see *her*—but at this moment, no one was looking out the window. Moving swiftly and silently, Amy hurried past the desk and into the stairwell. She walked down a couple of flights and came out in a hall where no one would recognize her. There she took the elevator to the ground level. There was a receptionist at the information desk in the lobby, plus a couple of people in security uniforms, and Amy had to pass them to get to the main doors. She held her breath.

But nobody even glanced at her as she went out into the night.

# sx

The silence and gloom of the black night were pierced by the wail of an ambulance and its flashing red lights. It turned the corner. Seconds later, the siren fell silent, and the quiet darkness became once again like a thick wool blanket, the kind you wanted to kick off on a warm summer night.

Amy quickened her pace as she walked along a street where there were no signs of life. This had to be a business district. All she could see were vacant office buildings and empty parking lots.

A bright red sports car careened onto the street and slowed down. The driver leaned over and spoke to Amy through the open window. "Hi, honey. Looking for a date?" His eyebrows moved up and down in a disgusting wiggle.

Amy was shocked. What kind of creep would speak to a kid like that? Then she remembered—she wasn't a kid. She was an attractive young woman walking alone on a deserted street.

Keeping her eyes firmly focused ahead, she started walking faster. The man got the message and drove away. A few minutes later, she spotted a police car coming in her direction. She stiffened and considered running— but the officer in the car just glanced at her without much curiosity. Why would he be concerned about an adult woman who wasn't breaking any laws? Even if it *was* after midnight. She could stay out as long as she wanted and the police wouldn't question her. In the strangest way, she felt relieved and at the same time a little sad.

The problem was, she didn't really want to stay out much longer. She was tired, and she was hungry. She'd been walking like this, rapidly, for over an hour now, trying to put as much distance as possible between herself and the hospital. Because of her superior physical endurance, she knew that if she put a little effort into it she could keep moving for a long time. She just didn't *feel* like it. Maybe because she had no idea what she was walking toward. She needed a destination.

But where could she go? It wasn't like she could suddenly appear at a friend's door. No one would recognize her, and even if she could convince someone that she was really Amy Candler, how would she explain the change in her appearance? Tasha and Eric were the only ones who might possibly understand, but they'd be up north at their camp by now.

Way off in the distance, she thought she saw the light of a taxi. She could hail it and tell the driver to take her to a hotel. But then something occurred to her.

She opened her bag and took out her wallet. It was just as she feared: There were two dollar bills and assorted change. There was probably more at the bottom of the bag, but nothing substantial. She could forget about taxis and hotels. She might have enough for a bus, but she didn't even know if buses ran this late.

Was it her imagination, or was she hearing the sound of a bus right now? Yes, it was a bus, and she could identify the direction. It had to be at least half a mile away, though. Now she was grateful that there was no one around. She broke into her fastest run, and no one saw the passing blur.

The bus was just starting to pull away as Amy reached it, but she pounded on the door and she lucked out. The kindly driver stopped. He didn't even complain as Amy took forever counting out the right change for the fare. She began to feel more optimistic—even though she didn't know where the bus was going. She looked up at a sign and read the destination: Hollywood, Sunset Boulevard. Well, that was a relief. She didn't know Hollywood well, but she'd been on Sunset before. The Strip, it was called, and she knew she'd see some people there.

Sure enough, Sunset was alive with bright lights, flashing neon signs, and lots of noise, and her spirits rose. People of all types, young and old, strolled the sidewalks, going in and out of restaurants and supper clubs, discos, fast-food joints, arcades, and bars. Each time a door opened, Amy could hear music and laughter and loud conversation. Some of the places seemed kind of trashy. Other places looked very fancy and expensive, and crowds of dressed-up people waited in front to get into them.

She spotted a place that didn't look either too fancy or too crummy and went inside. At the bar, she asked the man for a soft drink. The place wasn't very crowded, but it didn't look like it was going to close down anytime soon, and there was air-conditioning. She could stay here for a while and figure out what her next step would be.

Her soda appeared. "That'll be four even," the man said.

"Four dollars?" she repeated faintly. "For a Coke?"

"That's the price, miss."

Amy put her money on the bar, and the man looked at it. "That's not enough," he told her.

"It's all I've got," she said.

He removed the soda. "This isn't a charitable institution, lady."

"How much for water?" she asked without much hope.

He gave her a look that basically told her to clear out.

Back out on the Strip, the scene didn't appear quite so cheerful anymore. There were still people around, but they all seemed to have places to go, money to spend. And they weren't alone. *She* was alone. And here, in a crowd, she felt even more alone than she'd felt on the deserted streets.

Had her absence been noticed back at the hospital? Probably. And her mother would have been alerted right away. She would be in a panic now. Amy refused to feel bad about that. If her mother had only listened to her, she wouldn't have needed to run off like this.

Her mind full of thoughts, Amy didn't see the outstretched legs on the pavement and almost tripped over them. "Oh! Excuse me!"

A boy sitting with his back against a wall glared at her. He looked about her age—well, the age she used to be. "Are you okay?" she asked.

"No," he said. "You got any money? I'm hungry."

So was she. But he looked worse off. She could practically see his ribs poking out from under his T-shirt.

She went into her purse and pulled out one of her two dollar bills. "Here." He took it wordlessly, without even a thank-you. Suddenly, out of nowhere, another boy appeared, and Amy had the sinking suspicion she was about to give away her last dollar. Before he could even ask, she thrust the bill at him. "I know, you're hungry too. Here, take it."

But this boy had eyes only for the kid sitting on the sidewalk. "Hey, man, you want a place to sleep?"

Stuffing the bill Amy had given him in his pocket, the boy got up. "Nah." He shuffled off.

Amy looked at the boy who'd made the offer. He was just as thin as the other boy, but he looked cleaner. Younger, too—maybe only ten or eleven. His straight blond hair hung almost to his shoulders and practically covered half his face. He wore faded jeans and a white T-shirt with SANCTUARY scrawled across the front.

He'd frowned when his offer was rejected, but when he caught Amy's eye, he just shrugged. "Some people, you can't help them."

Impulsively Amy spoke. "You can help *me*. I need a place to sleep."

He shook his head. "Sorry. Sanctuary doesn't take anyone over fifteen. But I think there's a homeless shelter near here."

"What's Sanctuary?" Amy asked.

"It's a place for kids to hang."

"Runaways?"

"Some of us are runaways. Look, I'm on duty tonight, I can't hang around. Gotta keep moving."

But this was the first nice human contact Amy had had for a while, and she wasn't going to let him go so easily. She walked beside him. "Where'd you run away from?" she asked.

"Up north," he replied vaguely.

"You ever think about going back?"

"No."

She tried to show him that she was sympathetic. "I guess you didn't get along with your parents, huh? I can relate to that. My mother doesn't—I mean, when I was your age, my mother didn't understand me."

He looked at her through narrowed eyes. Then he lifted a lock of the hair that hung down over his face.

Amy gasped. A long scar ran along his cheek. "What happened to you?"

"My father's girlfriend. She tried to cut off my ear."

Appalled, Amy stared at the jagged pink line. "Why?"

"She said I never listened to her."

"Didn't your father try to stop her?"

"Are you kidding? He would have helped her, but he was too drunk to stand up."

Amy felt sick. "That's awful."

He shrugged. "It's nothing compared to some of the stories I hear."

"At Sanctuary?"

He nodded.

They walked along in silence for a moment. "What's your name?" Amy asked.

"Max."

"I'm Amy," she said. "Can you tell me some more about Sanctuary?"

He looked at her sharply. "Why?"

She wondered why he was being so suspicious. Then she caught a glimpse of the two of them in a store window. A boy of about ten or eleven and an adult woman. No wonder he didn't trust her. "I never heard of this place, Sanctuary," she said.

His eyes narrowed. "You're not a cop, are you?"

Amy was startled. "No! Is Sanctuary illegal or something?"

"Nah, but we like to keep a low profile. We're not exactly official. It's a private place. Not one of those holes that are run by the city."

"Who runs it?" Amy asked.

"A couple. Brother James and Sister Karen."

Amy wrinkled her nose. "What is it, some kind of religious cult?"

Max almost smiled. "No, nothing like that. But we don't use any last names. They just use these titles, Brother and Sister, to show that they're in charge."

"How come they don't just call themselves Mother and Father?"

" 'Cause a lot of kids at Sanctuary don't get good feelings when they hear words like *Mother* and *Father*."

Amy shivered. She knew there were a lot of kids in the world who hadn't lucked out when it came to parents. Even so, it was creepy to think about.

"Anyway," Max continued, "they don't want to sound like authority figures. I mean, they're in charge, but they don't push us around, you know?"

"Are they nice?"

For the first time, she saw a real smile on Max's face. "Yeah, they're great. They started this place on their

own, and they don't make any money from it or anything. They use their own money to feed us, and they
give us beds and clothes."

"How many of you are there?"

"Right now, seven of us are staying at Sanctuary."

"Wow. And that couple, they pay for everyone?"

"Yeah. Because they care about kids like us."

Amy thought for a minute. "I care about kids like
you. Do you think Brother James and Sister Karen
could use any help?"

He looked at her appraisingly. "I guess you could
meet them."

It was a good thing Max was with her. She would
never have been able to find the place on her own.
It was on a side street, and the entrance was a metal
door with no identifying sign on it. Max banged on
the door.

Amy noticed a tiny hole in the door, and she could
tell that someone was looking out. Then the door
opened.

The girl who stood there was maybe a year or two
older than Max. Her hair was an unnatural black, and
she'd used gel or something to make it stand up in
straight spikes. There didn't seem to be any part of her
body that wasn't pierced. Silver rings dangled from

her ears, eyebrows, nose, and lips. When she opened her mouth, Amy could see a silver post in the middle of her tongue.

She nodded at Max, but when she saw Amy behind him, her expression turned hostile. "Who's *she?*"

"She wants to meet Brother James and Sister Karen."

That didn't change the girl's face. "Why? What does she want?"

Max didn't answer. "So, where are they?"

"Brother James is out looking for kids. Sister Karen's in the laundry room."

"C'mon," Max said to Amy. He led her up a narrow metal staircase. "Don't mind Liz, she acts like that to every stranger."

"Liz was the girl who let us in?"

"Yeah. A lot of strangers haven't treated her too good, if you know what I mean."

Amy wasn't sure she did, and she wasn't sure she wanted to know, either. When they reached the landing, they were in a large, loftlike space. In one area sat a worn-looking sofa and some beat-up chairs. The rug on the floor was thin, but there were brightly colored large pillows scattered over it. What looked like homemade shelves lined one wall, and they overflowed with books. There were also a small TV and a portable cassette player. At the other end stood a large wooden table surrounded by metal folding chairs.

"That's where we eat. Kitchen's just beyond it. Beds are upstairs." Amy looked around as she followed him through the space. The room and its furnishings were shabby, but the place looked nice and cozy. A big poster on the wall read TODAY IS THE FIRST DAY OF THE REST OF YOUR LIFE.

The stove and refrigerator in the kitchen looked like they were a hundred years old, but everything was very clean. Through a door off the kitchen, Amy could hear the rumble of a washing machine.

"Sister Karen?" Max called.

The door opened and revealed a woman whose dark hair was pulled back severely in a ponytail. She looked like she was in her twenties. My age, Amy thought.

"Hi, Max." Sister Karen smiled warmly, but her eyebrows went up when she realized Max wasn't alone.

"This is Amy," Max said. "She wants to work at Sanctuary."

The woman came out of the laundry room. She was still smiling, but she eyed Amy warily. "We're not hiring anyone to work here."

"I'm not looking for a job," Amy said hastily. "I mean, not a paying job. I just want to help. You know, like a volunteer."

The woman still didn't look very encouraging. "Why do you want to volunteer here, at Sanctuary?"

"Because . . . because . . ." Amy was at a loss for words. "Because it seems like a nice place," she finished lamely.

Sister Karen gazed at her steadily. Then she turned to the boy. "Max, where's Robbie?"

"He didn't come out with me on patrol. Said he was too tired."

The woman frowned. "Max, you know you're not supposed to patrol the streets on your own. If Robbie couldn't go with you, you should have come to me or Brother James, and we would have sent someone else with you. And if we couldn't find anyone to go with you, you wouldn't have gone at all."

"I can handle the streets on my own," Max said roughly, but Sister Karen shook her head.

"It's one of our rules, Max, you know that. And if you're going to be a member of the Sanctuary family, you have to obey our family rules. Or you can't be part of the family." She spoke gently but firmly, and suddenly Max looked frightened.

"Are you throwing me out?" he asked.

She smiled. "No, Max, we believe in second chances. Just try not to break any more rules, okay?"

Relief swept over the boy's face. "Okay."

"You're looking pretty wiped out," Sister Karen said. "Why don't you go on up to bed?"

"Okay. 'Night."

"Good night," Sister Karen said, and Amy echoed that. Max left the kitchen, and Sister Karen beckoned for Amy to follow her into the main room. She motioned toward a chair at the dining table, and Amy sat down. Sister Karen sat across from her and gazed at Amy. Her eyes were light blue, and even though she looked tired, she was beautiful.

"I appreciate your interest, Amy," she said. "But this place—it's not like a nursing home, where you can show up for a couple of hours each week. Sanctuary isn't like most charitable organizations or shelters. For one thing, we're a completely residential community. A family. My husband, James, and I live here with the kids. This is our home as well as theirs. I don't think we'd be comfortable with volunteers who come and go. We're totally committed to this place. Sanctuary is our whole life."

"Could it be my whole life too?" Amy asked. "I wouldn't have to come and go. I could just . . . *stay*."

"You mean, live here with us?"

Amy nodded.

"But don't you have a home? A family?"

Amy hesitated. The girl Amy Candler had a home, of course. And a mother. But the person she was now, the woman she had become—this Amy belonged nowhere, belonged to no one. She felt like she could answer, in total honesty, "No. No home, no family." After a second she said, "I guess you want to ask me a lot of questions."

To her surprise, Sister Karen shook her head. "No, we try not to ask too many questions here. We tell each other what we want to share. The past is past; we don't dwell on the bad things that have happened to us. That's what we tell the kids who come to stay here. At Sanctuary they're safe, and they can make a new beginning."

Amy glanced toward the poster on the wall. " 'Today is the first day of the rest of your life,' " she read out loud.

"Exactly," Sister Karen said. And for the first time, her smile seemed completely open and sincere.

"Is that what you tell the volunteers, too?" Amy asked. Because it sounded to her like this was exactly what *she* needed: a place where she could start her new life.

"We've never had any volunteers," Sister Karen told her.

"You mean, you do everything yourself?" Amy was impressed. "You and Brother James? You take care of all the kids staying here?"

Sister Karen nodded. "And cook, and clean, and organize . . . you name it."

"Sounds like you could use some help," Amy said.

There was the sound of heavy footsteps on the stairs, and a tall man came in. He looked around the same age as Sister Karen, and he too had dark hair pulled back in a ponytail. But his eyes weren't blue. They were dark, and as he came closer to Amy, they got even darker.

"Who are you?" he asked abruptly. "What are you doing here?"

Sister Karen answered for her. "This is Amy, James. She wants to work with us here at Sanctuary."

His expression didn't exactly say "Welcome." He stared at her, and those intense dark eyes radiated distrust.

"What's the deal?" he asked. "Who are you? Someone's relative? A private investigator? Who sent you? Which kid are you after?"

He practically spit the questions at her, and Amy was momentarily overwhelmed. But she pulled herself together and faced him squarely.

"I'm not after anyone, and no one sent me, and I'm just a regular person."

He didn't appear to be convinced. But Karen spoke up. "I think she's okay, James. I'm getting good vibes from her. I think she's for real."

"I *am* for real," Amy said stoutly. "And I want to live and work here. Because I know what it's like to be a kid with problems."

He looked at her doubtfully. "You were abused?"

"Not exactly," Amy said. "Not like Max. But—but I wasn't treated very well. Things—things were done to me. . . ."

"What kind of things?"

"James, I told her she wouldn't have to answer questions about her past," Karen said, but James didn't relent.

"What was so terrible about your childhood?" he asked.

"I was—I was different. They put me in a hospital and tested me and poked me and hooked me up to machines. And I wasn't even sick. But they wouldn't let me out. So I ran away."

Was there a change in Brother James's eyes? Did they suddenly become warmer? "How old were you when this happened?"

Amy swallowed. "Thirteen."

"And you've been on your own ever since?"

She nodded. He looked at Sister Karen, who smiled sadly at him. "Sound familiar?" she asked.

He nodded and turned back to Amy. "I was fifteen," he murmured. His dark eyes bored into her. Then he smiled.

"All right. You can stay."

# se7en

At four o'clock in the afternoon, most of the campers were down by the lake. Eric was on a break. He would have preferred to be at the lake with the six nine-year-olds from his cabin, but the senior counselor, Steve, had told him to get lost.

"You got a Red Cross lifesaving certificate?" he'd asked Eric. Eric had to admit that no, he didn't have any official certificate. He was a good swimmer, and the lake was shallow, but according to Steve, only certified lifesavers were allowed to hang out during waterfront activities.

Eric doubted that this was a camp rule. All the senior

counselors were certified, but when he asked a couple of the other junior counselors, he discovered that they didn't have any special training. And the senior counselors they worked with let them go in the canoes with the campers.

Maybe Steve just wanted to get rid of him. That wouldn't surprise Eric. They'd gotten off on the wrong foot when Eric had first arrived, three days earlier. Eric had helped Tasha carry her bags over to the girls' side and had spent more time with her than he'd realized. She was in major need of a pep talk about how camp could turn out to be okay, don't be a wimp, give it a chance, blah, blah, blah. So by the time Eric arrived at the boys' camp, he was a little late, and the campers and counselors were already at dinner.

Eric had gone to dump his own bags in his cabin and had been surprised to find a lone camper there. The poor kid was crying. Of course, he was humiliated when Eric saw him blubbering, but Eric tried to be cool about it. He told the kid he himself had been totally freaked the first time he went away to a sleepover camp, and that it was normal to be homesick the first day.

The boy went with him to the lodge where the campers ate. Eric met Steve and tried to explain why he was late, but Steve was totally unsympathetic.

"Listen, kid, one of your major responsibilities is to

monitor the mealtimes—make the kids eat their vegetables and stop any food fights. You better not be late again." And Steve barked and yelled at the younger boy, who was still sniffling, and told him not to be a crybaby. Which only made the kid feel worse.

When Eric had been a kid at camp, the counselors had all been pretty nice. But there was always a rotten one in the bunch. Here it looked like it would be Steve.

Eric ambled around the campgrounds, trying to think of something to do, and remembered seeing some computer terminals in the lodge. He could always go and check his e-mail.

Except for the camp secretary in her office, the lodge was empty. He sat down at one of the terminals and logged on to his Internet service provider. He entered his user name and his password, and he waited. There was nothing, which wasn't really a surprise. His parents would send old-fashioned snail mail, and his buds were on vacations where they would have better things to do than write e-mails.

But Amy should have written by now. Was she still in the hospital? he wondered. Was she too sick to write? No, he comforted himself, she probably just didn't have access to a computer there. At least he could make sure an e-mail was waiting for her when she got home. He hit Compose Mail, typed in her address, and began to write.

*Amy: I don't know where you are or what's going on. I hope you get this. I'm here at camp, and being a junior counselor isn't exactly what I thought it would be. According to Steve, the senior counselor in my cabin, all I have to do is prevent the kids from killing each other. I haven't even had to break up a fight.*

*The kids are okay, but I feel sorry for some of them. It's like their parents have sent them here to get rid of them. Some kids are really homesick. This one kid told me that his parents wanted to go off on some fancy cruise by themselves so they stuck him here. Another kid's parents are divorced, and his mother wants to go out on dates, and she doesn't want her boyfriends to see that she's got a nine-year-old son because that might scare the guys away. Pretty sick, huh? I keep hearing these really sad stories, and it's kind of depressing. So I said to Steve, maybe we could have some bull sessions, you know, where the kids can sit around a campfire and talk about their feelings and stuff. And Steve says, no way, we don't get paid enough to be psychologists. It's weird, he's probably only about seven years older than me, but I guess that makes him an adult.*

*What happens when people get older? It's like they*

can't remember how they used to feel. Your mother wouldn't let me visit you, or even call you, and I don't think she was telling me the whole truth about what was going on. My parents wouldn't even listen to me when I told them I didn't want to go to camp till you got back from the hospital. I guess no one takes you seriously until you're over twenty-one or something. And then you become one of them, and you forget what it was like to be a kid.

I hope you're okay. I miss you.

Eric


He did a spell check, and he was just about to send the note off when he moved the cursor. After *I miss you,* he inserted *a lot.* And before *Eric,* he typed *love.*

# e**i**ght

It was after two in the morning, and it was raining, so there weren't as many people as usual on Sunset Boulevard. Amy tried to keep at least half a block behind Max and Robbie. Sister Karen had told her that street kids might be put off by the sight of an adult recruiting for Sanctuary. They were much more likely to open up to kids their own age. "They won't trust an adult," Karen had said. "They've been let down by too many adults before."

The past few days at Sanctuary had been a real revelation to Amy. Of course, she had known that there were mistreated children in the world. She'd heard about mentally disturbed parents who actually murdered their own children. She'd read reports about child abuse in the newspapers, she'd seen movies about the subject, and she was aware that there were a lot of sick people and sad, even tragic stories.

But now she was meeting actual victims. They had names; she could see their faces; she could hear their stories from their own lips. And she could understand why Sister Karen and Brother James had devoted themselves to helping these kids find some relief, some comfort.

"They have no rights," Brother James had been saying to her and Karen just the night before. "No one protects them. Parents pretty much own their kids. It's like the olden days on the plantations down south. The parent is the master, and the kid is a slave."

Karen had objected to that broad generalization. "There are some good parents out there, James. Not all kids are treated like slaves."

James brushed her objection aside. "You can't tell me there aren't an awful lot of slaves out there too. When I think of what some of these parents have done to their kids . . ." His mouth was set in a grim line. "Amy, I'm not a violent person by nature, but sometimes, when I think of what these kids have been through, I start fantasizing about what I'd like to do to the adults who were responsible for them." He clenched his fists, and real fire burned in his eyes. Amy had no trouble imagining what he might be capable of doing.

"It's ironic, isn't it?" Karen said. "A person has to get a license to drive a car. You have to take a written test, and a road test, and prove to the authorities that you can handle a car and drive correctly. But practically any man or woman, no matter how incompetent or mean or worthless they might be, can get together and make a baby. Even if they know absolutely nothing about raising a child."

They'd all been feeling particularly emotional about this the night before, because a new girl had joined the Sanctuary family. In a way, it had been Amy's initiation. She was the one who had found Lisa and brought her in.

Amy had been out on the streets by herself, wandering around and familiarizing herself with the area. It was in the middle of the afternoon, broad daylight, and she'd been watching through a store window as a couple of teenage shoplifters were caught. The girls were guilty, she could see that, but she wondered if it was really necessary for the security guard to put handcuffs on them and treat them like hardened criminals. She was just considering using her adult status to make an official complaint when someone approached her.

"Are you Dollface?"

Amy turned and faced a short, stocky girl with curly brown hair. She looked about fourteen years old. "What?"

The girl was clearly nervous. Her eyes darted from side to side. "Are you the one they call Dollface?"

Amy responded cautiously. "What if I am?"

"Look, I gotta know," the girl said urgently. "If you're Dollface, I got something for you. From Marla."

"Okay," Amy said. "Yeah, I'm Dollface."

The girl slipped off the backpack that hung down her back and started to unzip it. Then she stopped. "Wait a minute. How do I know you're really Dollface?"

Amy tried to look tough. "You want to see my driver's license?"

"Yeah."

Amy faltered. "Well . . . you can't. 'Cause I don't have it with me. But I'm really Dollface, so give me what Marla sent."

The girl stared at her. "Tell me Marla's last name."

"What is this?" Amy asked. "A test?"

"Yeah."

Amy hesitated, and the girl zipped the pack back up. "Never mind."

"What are you selling?" Amy asked.

"I'm not selling," the girl muttered. "I'm delivering. What are you, a cop?"

"No," Amy said. "What are you, a dealer?" As the girl turned away, Amy grabbed her arm. "Tell me. Are you dealing drugs?"

Now the girl looked frightened. She tried to pull away, but Amy tightened her grasp, and there was no way the girl could break free. "Look, I swear, I'm not a cop. I'm not going to arrest you."

"I don't believe you," the girl said through her teeth.

"You see that trash can over there?" Amy asked her. "Why don't you toss that backpack? Then you and I can go someplace and talk."

"Are you crazy?" the girl demanded. "You know what Dollface would do?"

"No. What would Dollface do?"

"Well, she'd tell Marla I didn't deliver the stuff."

"And what would Marla do?"

The girl hesitated. Finally she said, "She'd throw me out of the house. I'll be sleeping on the streets."

"Is Marla your mother?"

The girl's eyes were bitter. "She might as well be."

Just then a hard-looking woman with frizzy dyed red hair approached them.

"Marla sent you?"

The girl nodded. The woman grabbed the backpack and walked away.

"I guess that was Dollface," Amy remarked.

"Hope so," the girl said. Her shoulders slumped, as if she still had the weight of the backpack on them.

"Wanna talk?" Amy asked.

The girl didn't say yes and she didn't say no. But she fell into step beside Amy, and they walked together.

Back at Sanctuary, with Brother James and Sister Kate, Amy heard the whole ugly story. The girl's name was Lisa. It turned out that Marla was her aunt, and when both of Lisa's parents had been killed in a car accident, Marla had inherited her brother's insurance money. She also inherited Lisa, and she wasn't too happy about that.

"That was a year ago," Lisa told them. "She's an addict, so the insurance money didn't last long. She's had me doing her deliveries ever since. She says that's the way I can pay her back for my bed and my meals." Lisa was trying to act tough, but her voice was faltering, and after a few more minutes, her hard shell cracked completely. She cried in Karen's arms.

Brother James had listened to the story without

comment. But when Lisa broke down, so did he. In his anger, he hit the wall with his fist. The next morning at breakfast, Amy could see the black-and-blue bruises on his knuckles.

Lisa was safe now, at Sanctuary. Her aunt wouldn't dare come looking for her. And Lisa knew she had a place to stay, so she wouldn't hesitate to turn Marla in to the police.

But Lisa was just a drop in the bucket. There were so many other kids in trouble out there. At that very moment, just ahead, Amy saw Max and Robbie talking to a boy. Either he was very short for his age, or he was very young. As Amy slowly approached, she realized he couldn't be more than ten.

Max beckoned for her to join them. "This is Evan. He lives in a foster home."

"Sounds more like a torture chamber to me," Robbie muttered.

"Where are your parents?" Amy asked him.

"My father's dead," Evan said. "My mother's in jail." He didn't look particularly bothered by that, and he confirmed this impression with his next words. "The old bag killed the old man."

"So Evan got sent to the foster home from hell," Max said.

Evan shrugged. "It's not as bad as the last one. At

least I can get out for a few hours every day." He offered a halfhearted grin. "They got this ladder out back right against the wall. I sneak out through my window."

"Why can't you sneak out the front door?" Amy asked.

"They lock me in my room. See, they get a lot of money from the state for keeping foster kids. So they don't want me running off. Besides, they need me. Who else is going to collect the empty whiskey bottles and put them in the recycling bin?"

Amy felt sick. It was just like Brother James said—another master-and-slave situation. At least this master wasn't the slave's real parent.

"I told him about Sanctuary," Max told Amy. "But he doesn't want to come with us."

"I can't leave the others," Evan said sadly.

Amy moaned. "There are other foster kids there?"

Even nodded. "Little ones. Four-year-old twins. And a baby. I'm the only one who talks to the twins. I tell 'em stories at night—they'd never go to sleep without me. And the baby, they hardly ever change his diaper. *I* do that."

It was a nightmare. And then Amy realized that both Max and Robbie were looking up at her, as if expecting her to decide how to deal with this. She had to remind herself that she was the adult among them.

"Come with us back to Sanctuary," she said to Evan. "We'll tell Brother James the story, and he'll figure out a way to get you all out of there."

Evan faltered. "I won't stay at Sanctuary," he warned her. "I won't abandon the kids."

"Neither will we," Amy assured him.

As they approached the side street where Sanctuary was, a man in a hooded raincoat came out onto the main street. He didn't look at them, but Amy found herself staring at his back.

"Have any of you guys seen that man before?" she asked.

"I didn't see him *now*," Robbie replied. "And neither did you. His face was covered."

Robbie's ordinary eyes couldn't have registered the man's face in that brief half second when his profile had been visible. But Amy had seen it, and her photographic memory immediately focused on the crooked nose and the sunken chin. She knew she'd seen that profile before. But it could have been anywhere, just walking down a street, so she put it out of her mind and concentrated on Evan's situation.

Brother James, of course, confirmed to Evan what Amy had said. "We're going to get all of you out of there," he stated firmly. "We'll break in if we have to. If they're as drunk all the time as you say, they won't be able to stop us."

But Sister Karen wasn't quite so sure. "We're talking about really young children here, James. Maybe we should alert the authorities."

James scowled. "Yeah, and let those kids get caught up in the city bureaucracy. They'll end up in a file, in the back of a cabinet. It could take those social workers weeks to investigate. Once they do, they'll just stick the kids in another crummy foster home."

"Not all foster homes are crummy," Karen murmured. "Some people become foster parents because they really care."

James gave her a stony look. Then he turned back to Evan. "Tell me about this ladder out back."

As a rescue plan was formulated, Amy could feel the excitement rise within her. This was like something out of a movie—they had a mission. It was thrilling, and it might even be dangerous. James wanted Amy to go with him. Karen would stay behind. They never left Sanctuary without one adult to supervise.

"But how are you going to get two four-year-olds and a baby away from the house?" Karen asked. "They might be crying or screaming. You're going to run all the way back here carrying them?"

"No," James said. "We'll take a car."

Karen stared at him. "James, we don't have a car."

"We'll borrow one," James replied.

"Oh, James, no," Karen moaned. "Not again. You could get caught this time. It's against the law!"

But James didn't seem to care. "Desperate situations call for desperate acts" was all he said.

When she walked out of the building with Evan and James, Amy recalled the man she'd seen when she came in. "Brother James, have you ever noticed a man hanging around here? He's got a crooked nose and not much of a chin."

"I haven't seen him," James said. "Why, did he bother you?"

"No. I'm just trying to figure out where I saw him before—if it was around here or just on a street."

"We do get some people lurking around," James told her. "Once, a rich family hired a private investigator to find their daughter, who was hiding out with us. He could be someone like that. Let me know if you see him again." He stopped walking and looked at a station wagon that was parked at the curb. "This would work. It looks like a family-style car. And it's so old, it probably doesn't have an alarm."

Evan peered through a window. "There's even a baby seat in the back."

"Excellent," James said. He went over to the driver's

side and took a small instrument out of his pocket. It looked like a tiny screwdriver. He crouched down and examined the lock on the door.

Amy knew what he was trying to do, and she tried not to be shocked. Clearly, Brother James had done this before. He fiddled around for a while, and then Amy heard a little pop. James opened the door and jumped into the driver's seat. Leaning over, he unlocked the passenger side and the back door.

Brother James used another little instrument to get the motor started, and they pulled away from the curb. Evan directed James to the house where he had been living, which didn't take long to reach. James parked across the street from the small two-story cottage with its peeling paint and broken shutters. Amy could see a light through a first-floor window.

"Are they awake?" she wondered aloud.

"Sometimes they're so drunk they can't even get up the stairs," Evan told her. "They fall asleep in front of the TV. The kids'll be upstairs, though. They get locked in right after they're fed. *If* they're fed."

He led them around to the back and pointed out the ladder that leaned against the wall. "Let me go up and get them," he said. "They'll recognize me and they won't be frightened."

Amy watched Evan climb the ladder. As he stepped on a certain rung, she could hear a squeaking that made her nervous. The ladder was in pretty bad shape, and it didn't look like it could bear much weight. Fortunately, Evan didn't look like he weighed a lot.

He squeezed through a window that only a small person could fit through. But his size could be a disadvantage, too, as Amy clearly saw when he reappeared at the window with two sleepy children in his arms.

"You can't bring them both down together!" she said to him urgently, but keeping her voice down. But Evan couldn't hear her, and she didn't dare speak any more loudly.

James could see the danger too. He moved closer to the bottom of the ladder. "One at a time, Evan!" But apparently Evan couldn't hear him, either. With one kid under each arm, he tried to get both of his feet on a rung. The ladder wobbled, and Evan wobbled too, trying to keep his balance while holding the kids.

James jumped onto the ladder and started climbing, but now the ladder was making ominous groaning noises. He put his weight on one rung, and it cracked loudly. It broke, and he had to struggle to get his footing on the next rung up. He met Evan halfway up and took one of the twins. He climbed down and handed the dazed-looking child to Amy. Evan was coming down with the other one. Another rung cracked, and while grabbing the rail, Evan jostled the child. The twin immediately began to wail like a siren, and he was thrashing about so hard that Evan was having a tough time holding on.

James jumped back onto the ladder to help Evan down, but this time his weight was too much. As he put his foot on the third rung, there was a sharp noise. James fell to the ground with a thud.

"Are you okay?" Amy asked anxiously. He was—but now there was something else to worry about. A light came on in the cottage next door, and a second later an angry voice could be heard.

"Shut up out there! Do you know what time it is?"

Evan lowered himself to a point where Amy could take the second twin from him. Then he started back up for the baby. But now the ladder had had enough. There was a wrenching, cracking sound, and the ladder started coming down. Fortunately for Evan, he wasn't that far up, and the fall didn't hurt him.

Now both twins were screaming. "Let's get out of here!" James said.

"What about the baby?" Amy asked.

"There's nothing we can do, Amy!" Evan said. "I can't get back up to the second floor!"

But Amy could. And for once, she didn't care about people witnessing her amazing abilities. She stepped back and took a flying leap. She managed to grip the top of the ground-floor window frame and swung her legs around. Her feet could just catch the bottom of the second-story window. But that was enough for her. With concentration and real exertion, she used her toehold to hoist herself up into the window and dropped into the room. She scooped the baby out of her crib and went back to the window.

For a moment Amy thought she'd been deserted by the others. Then James came running around to the back of the house, and she realized that they must have taken the twins to the car. James looked up at her in fear and concern.

"You'll have to jump!" he called. "Throw the baby down, I'll catch her!"

With her keen eyesight, Amy could see James on the ground, his arms outstretched. But she also realized that he couldn't see her or the baby. There was very little chance that he'd be able to catch the infant.

Then she heard a voice on the other side of the bedroom door. "Hey, what's going on?" a man was yelling. She could hear a key turning in the lock. Amy had no choice. Clutching the baby close, she climbed out the window. And she jumped.

She hit the ground with a thud, but she stayed on her feet. Her real fear was for the baby, who gasped on the way down.

But then the infant opened her mouth and let out a piercing cry. She might have been scared out of her mind, but she was alive.

James was staring at Amy in disbelief, but there was no time for explanations. A man was at the upstairs window. "I'm calling the police!" he screamed.

Amy took off with the baby, and James was just behind her. In the car, Evan held the twins in the back. Amy ran around to the passenger side while James got behind the wheel. This time he had a little more difficulty getting the car started, and Amy held her breath, expecting to hear a police siren at any moment.

But in a few seconds the reassuring sound of the motor kicked in and they took off. The baby had stopped crying, and the twins were quiet too. Nobody said a word until they reached the street where they'd taken the car.

And then they had a real stroke of luck. The parking space was still vacant. James lined the car up and executed a perfect parallel park.

Out on the street, Evan held the hand of each twin

while Amy cradled the baby. James looked at the car with real satisfaction. "Not even a scratch," he said proudly.

It was amazing, Amy thought as they all hurried down the side street with the kids. Whoever owned that car would never know what a good deed it had performed.

# nine

A cluster of preteen girls walking along the dirt path stared at Eric as they passed him sitting on Tasha's cabin steps. As if on cue, they all began to giggle wildly. Eric tried to ignore them. What was the big deal? Couldn't a guy visit his own sister at her camp without creating a fuss?

At least Tasha should be glad to see him. He just hoped she wouldn't start crying. After a whole week at camp, she was probably ready to crack. In fact, he'd been surprised not to find her moping alone in the cabin, especially since the camp director had told him her group was riding horses. Tasha was scared of all large animals.

Eric could make out another group of girls coming up the path. In fact, he could hear them before he could see them, since they were giggling just like the other group. He turned his head and pretended to be looking in the opposite direction. That was why he didn't see Tasha before she saw him.

"What are *you* doing here?" she demanded. To her cabin mates, she said, "He's my brother."

He was uncomfortably aware of the other girls gaping at him. "I need to talk to you," he said gruffly. "Alone."

"Okay." Tasha turned to the others. "I'll be right back." She went with Eric across the path to a bench on the other side, and they sat down. "What's going on?" she asked anxiously. "Is there something wrong at home? Are Mom and Dad okay?"

"Yeah, yeah, they're okay. It's me. I want to get out of here."

Tasha stared at him. "Why?"

"This place stinks," Eric blurted out. "I really hate it. Half the kids in my cabin are beating up on the other half. The senior counselor, Steve, is a total jerk. He doesn't care about the kids. All he wants to do is sunbathe and collect his paycheck. He won't even let me do any real counselor stuff. He's got me cleaning the cabin, for crying out loud! He treats me like scum."

"Yuck," Tasha commented. "In my cabin we all straighten up together. We have this chart, and we take turns dusting, sweeping, that sort of thing."

Eric wasn't interested in hearing about Tasha's cleaning regimen. "So I went to the director to complain," he continued. "He said if I don't like it here, I can leave. They don't really need the junior counselors. He even said I should count myself lucky because I'm getting a free bed, free meals, and a free camp experience."

"How's the food on your side?" Tasha asked. "It's not bad over here. The macaroni and cheese is excellent."

Eric frowned. He wasn't here to discuss camp cuisine. "Then Steve found out I talked to the director about him, so now he really has it in for me. He orders me around and yells at me in front of the little kids. It's no wonder they don't have any respect for me and won't listen to a thing I say. It's really a crummy place, Tasha. Half the kids are totally miserable, and the counselors don't even care."

"Gee, it's not like that around here," Tasha told him. "Our counselors are great, really cool. Like Martha in my cabin, she's been teaching us how to French-braid our hair. And in arts and crafts, we're learning to throw pots."

Eric had a vision of giggling girls tossing bowls at each other, and he couldn't understand why that would be appealing. He didn't want to know. "Look, I gotta get out of here. I'm thinking I'll call home."

"You're going to ask Mom and Dad to come get you?"

Eric hesitated. "Not exactly. I'll look like a real wimp, and they'll be pissed at me for not sticking it out. But if *you* wanted to come home, that would be different."

Tasha was puzzled. "Why?"

"Well, you didn't want to be here in the first place. And Mom and Dad already know you're a wimp. No offense," he added hastily as Tasha's expression darkened. "But you're not into sports and hiking and stuff like that. Anyway, you've been here a whole week, you gave it a chance, and that's all they really wanted you to do. I'll bet if you told them you hated this camp, they'd tell you to come home. Then I could offer to bring you, on a bus, so they wouldn't have to drive up."

He thought she would jump at the chance. He was surprised when she said, "But I don't hate it here."

"You don't?"

"No, I like it a lot better than I thought I would. A lot of the girls aren't superathletes, and no one teases anyone else. I love pottery, and next week we're going to paint the pots we've made. We're even going to have a talent show! I'm writing the skit for my cabin."

Eric was floored. "You don't want to leave?"

"No way. You should see me with Bingo!"

"Who's Bingo?"

"The horse I ride. He's so sweet, and he loves me! The riding counselor says I have an excellent seat."

He had no idea what she was talking about, but it didn't matter. The meaning was clear. Tasha liked camp; she didn't want to leave. Eric was not going to be able to use her as an excuse to get himself home.

He spoke glumly. "I gotta get back, it's almost time for lunch. That's one of my thrilling jobs, monitoring the kids while they eat and breaking up food fights. If I can't stop the fights, I have to clean up the mess."

"That stinks," Tasha said, and she sounded like she really meant it. But it was clear to him that her sympathy wouldn't extend to giving up her own camp experience. He supposed he should be pleased for his sister. But now he had no escape plan. He was stuck here.

He rose. "By the way, have you been checking your e-mail?"

"Yeah, every day."

"You heard anything from Amy?"

Tasha shook her head. "Mom said she saw Amy's

mother, though. And Ms. Candler said Amy's staying over at Dr. Hopkins's house for a while, so she can hang out at the beach."

Eric frowned. He couldn't picture Amy spending a week just lying around on the beach. And surely Dr. Hopkins had a computer at home. Amy should be able to check her account. So why hadn't she answered his e-mails?

"See ya," he said to Tasha, but she had already gone back into the cabin, and he could hear the giggles.

He certainly didn't feel like giggling himself. He seriously doubted that he'd even be able to muster up a smile for the next couple of weeks.

# ten 10

To Amy, Brother James looked like he hadn't been getting much sleep. Sitting across from her at the table during breakfast, he was pale, and there were dark circles under his eyes. Amy wasn't surprised. She too could hear baby Julie crying at night, and the infant was sleeping in the same room with James and Karen.

There was another reason why he looked gloomy. Brother James was doing what he usually did in the mornings at breakfast. He looked through the newspaper and pointed out items of interest to the other residents. Today the front page seemed to be getting him down even more than usual.

"What a world we live in," he said sadly. "Listen to this. 'Fire rages in high-rise apartment building. Firefighters blame lack of sprinklers.' Some cheap landlord was trying to cut corners, and now people are losing their homes. And how about this. 'Elementary school principal convicted on charges of child abuse.'" He let out a soft moan. "Ohmigod. 'Refugee stowaways on a boat suffocate in storage space. No survivors.'"

As if in response to all this tragic news, baby Julie started wailing again. She was lying beside the table in a makeshift cradle created out of a dresser drawer. James put a hand to his forehead and pressed his temples as if he was trying to squeeze a pain out of his head.

"Is she hungry?" he asked.

Liz shook her head. "I just fed her. And she isn't wet, I checked."

"Then why is she crying like that?" James asked irritably.

Liz shrugged. "Babies cry. That's what they do."

"I hope she's not sick," James said.

If she was, Amy knew, it could be a real problem. It wasn't like they could just take her to a doctor. There would be too many questions, and they couldn't draw public attention to Sanctuary. As both Brother James and Sister Karen reminded them all, they were operating outside the law.

"I don't think there's anything wrong with her," Lisa said. "She doesn't feel like she has a fever. And when I bathed her last night, I didn't see bruises or anything like that."

"Not all bruises are visible," James remarked. "Someone like Max, you could almost say he's lucky to have a real scar."

Max touched the side of his face. "I'm *lucky*?"

"Well, at least you've got clear evidence of being abused," James pointed out. "Some people only have psychological scars."

The way he said it made Amy think that maybe Brother James himself was carrying some deep scars where they couldn't be seen. She had a feeling that all the residents of Sanctuary carried black-and-blue marks in their hearts and minds.

Fourteen people were living here now. With the new arrivals, they'd all had to make space in the three bedrooms. Evan shared a space with Robbie and Max and three other boys between the ages of twelve and fifteen who had been at Sanctuary for a while. Amy, Liz, Lisa, and the four-year-old twins were crammed into another room. At least each of them had his or her own mattress or sleeping bag. It wasn't luxurious, but they had clean sheets and blankets and towels and plenty to eat. And it was all provided by Brother James and Sister Karen. Amy wondered how they could afford to do this. Neither of them had a job outside Sanctuary. They certainly didn't seem to be rich. Whatever they had, they shared with the residents of Sanctuary. It was hard to believe that such good, unselfish people existed.

The other member of the incredible couple entered the room at that moment. Sister Karen wasn't alone. She held the hand of a small, skinny, grimy-looking little girl.

"I found her by the harbor," Karen told them. "You know, where the fishing boats come in? I was buying some fresh tuna, and she wandered by. I waited, and I asked around, but no one seemed to be looking for her."

Amy knelt down and looked into the child's huge brown eyes. "Hello, I'm Amy. What's your name?"

The child just stared at her. She smelled awful, as if she hadn't had a bath in weeks.

"She hasn't said a word," Karen told her. "She's filthy, and I think she's hungry." She took a piece of toast from a basket on the dining table and handed it to the little girl. The child sniffed it, then wolfed it down hungrily. Karen went to the telephone and dialed.

"Could I speak with someone in Missing Persons? . . . Hello, I'd like to know if a child has been reported missing. She won't tell me her name, but she looks like she's about six years old. She's got short, straight black hair, brown eyes, and—" Karen wasn't able to provide any more description. James had rushed over to her. He grabbed the phone out of her hand and hung it up.

"What are you doing?" Karen asked in bewilderment.

"What are *you* doing?" he asked harshly.

"I'm trying to find out where this poor lost child belongs!"

"Look at her!" James cried out. "Do you want to give her back to the monsters who put her in that condition?"

Karen spoke reasonably and calmly. "James, she could have gotten that way on her own. We don't know that she was mistreated or abandoned. She could have wandered off. There might be caring parents who are worried sick right now."

"Caring parents would have watched their child more carefully," James thundered. "Any parent who can lose a child doesn't deserve to have one."

"James, be reasonable—"

"Shut up! Just shut up!"

Personally, Amy thought James sounded a little harsh. And he seemed suddenly to become aware of the silence in the room, as all the residents were listening to his argument with Karen. He stopped yelling.

"I'm sorry," he said to Karen. Amy thought he probably realized that too many of them came from homes where adults fought.

Karen nodded, seeming to accept the apology. "I'm going to clean her up," she said. She took the child out of the room.

Later, after the little girl had been bathed and fed and put to bed, Sister Karen sat down with Amy and Brother James to discuss the situation. "She still hasn't said anything. I thought she might have a hearing impairment, but she responds to noises."

"Maybe she doesn't speak English," James suggested.

"That's a possibility," Karen admitted. "I found a faded label inside her shirt, and it looks foreign."

"Let's give her a name!" Amy said brightly. James and Karen looked at her a little oddly, and she realized that under the circumstances, that was probably a silly suggestion. She was showing her own immaturity.

But then Karen smiled. "Well, we can't keep calling her 'she.' Okay, Amy, what would you like to name her?"

Amy thought. "How about Hope?"

"I like that," Karen said. Then she sighed. "Oh, James, I really feel like I should talk to the police. Some poor new immigrants who barely speak English could be absolutely frantic."

But later that day, as they watched the six o'clock news on TV, they learned little Hope's real name.

"We have more information on the tragic discovery of fifteen illegal refugees discovered in the hold of a supply ship this morning. The ship came from the island nation of Covalia, and the dead stowaways are all believed to be Covalian natives, attempting to escape from the oppressive military regime there. We have unconfirmed reports that among the original group was a child, the daughter of a couple who are among the dead. The child, six-year-old Vikna Doss, has not been accounted for. Covalian relatives hope that she may have survived, but authorities have been unable to locate her."

Amy knew they were all thinking the same thing, and she said it out loud. "Do you think Hope could be this Vikna Doss?"

Sister Karen nodded. "Where I found her . . . it wasn't far from where the ship came in. She could have survived in a tiny air pocket and slipped out unnoticed when the hold was opened."

"What a nightmare," Brother James said softly. "What that child has seen . . ."

"I've never heard of Covalia," Amy said. "Where is it?"

"In the Barren Sea," James told her. "It's a very poor country, with the worst human rights record in the world. It's run by a military dictatorship, and the government is totally corrupt. Vikna is lucky to be out of there."

"James, how can you call her lucky?" Karen cried out. "She lost her parents! They're dead!"

"At least they died trying to bring her to freedom," James said.

Karen looked at him beseechingly. "They must have been good people, James, to risk their lives like that. Those relatives the newscaster was talking about . . . they could be good people too. They're grieving now. Think what it would mean to them to know she's alive and well."

James was silent. He sighed deeply, and it sounded more like a groan. "All right. Let them know she's okay."

Karen ran to the phone and dialed. "Hello, I'm calling about the child, Vikna Doss, from the Covalian refugee ship. Please let her family know she survived, and that she's safe. What? My address?"

James leaped up. "Why do they want an address?"

"The Covalian embassy wants to send a representative to see her."

For the second time that day, James took the phone out of her hand and hung it up. "They're sending someone to take her away. And she's not going back."

# eleven

A my crouched down in front of the little girl sitting on the chair. "Vikna, let me tie your shoelaces."

Vikna looked at her blankly. Amy pointed to the shoe, and Vikna must have understood. Expressionless, she raised her foot, and Amy tied the laces. "There you go," she said brightly. "Now you won't trip."

Of course, the child didn't comprehend that, either. Amy wished she could find a dictionary that could teach her the language of Covalia. With her photographic memory, she would be able to learn at least some basic expressions quickly. She didn't know if it would do any good, though. She sensed that Vikna didn't want to communicate in any language.

The little girl hadn't spoken since she'd arrived at Sanctuary three days earlier. She hadn't cried, or laughed, or shown any sort of response to her surroundings. She didn't express hunger, thirst, or tiredness. If food was placed in front of her, she ate it. If she was laid down on a cot, she slept. But she never responded emotionally.

Sister Karen thought the child was in a state of shock, and Amy could easily believe that. She tried to imagine what it must have been like for Vikna, crammed in the hold of that ship. Had she been aware of each of her companions dying? Did she think they had just fallen asleep? What must it have been like for her when her mother and father didn't respond to her cries? It was too awful to contemplate.

Impulsively Amy hugged the little girl, but the child didn't hug back. Amy thought of those psychological scars James had talked about. She had an awful feeling that Vikna would be terribly scarred, deep inside where no one could see, and she hoped the child would be able to get lots of help from psychologists. Of course, that couldn't happen while she was at Sanctuary. Brother James wouldn't call in any doctors, since that would violate the secrecy of the place.

But Sanctuary wasn't a big secret anymore. In the past couple of days, people had begun to hear about it.

Liz yelled up from downstairs. "Amy, come quick! Sister Karen's on TV!"

Taking Vikna by the hand, Amy hurried out. In the main room, the TV set had been turned up full blast, and all the residents were gathered around. On the screen, Sister Karen looked pale and confused, but she spoke in a composed manner.

"I appreciate the fact that Vikna's relatives want her returned to Covalia. But the nation of Covalia is infamous for denying human rights to its citizens. Vikna's parents wanted their child to grow up in a country where she could be free. They risked their lives so their daughter could be brought here. As a memorial to her parents, we must allow Vikna to remain here in the United States and live free."

"Wow, this is wild!" Evan exclaimed, and the others started talking excitedly. Max stayed calm, but he was almost smiling.

The camera then switched to two solemn-looking TV newscasters sitting behind a desk. One of them said, "Once again, that was the woman who calls herself Sister Karen, speaking just over an hour ago as she was leaving the Sanctuary shelter. In response, the assistant deputy magistrate of Covalia has called a press conference to address the concern of the Doss family. We go live by satellite to Salzadar, Covalia."

An image of a man in a dark business suit filled the screen. "As a nation, we are outraged that the United States has not taken immediate steps to send Vikna Doss back to her family in Covalia," he said. "This child has blood relatives. They are her legal guardians now that her parents are deceased. She belongs with her family. The United States has no right to hold her hostage. We demand that this place known as Sanctuary release Vikna to the Covalian representative in the United States."

Robbie clenched his fists and made a threatening gesture toward the figure on the screen. "Oh yeah? Don't hold your breath, buddy! Vikna ain't going nowhere!"

The female newscaster was now speaking. "At a briefing on the Mideast in Washington, the secretary of state was asked about the Vikna Doss situation."

A woman at a podium was displayed on the screen. "We are currently attempting to learn more about the situation in Los Angeles. Local reports indicate that emergency citizenship has been requested for the child, and we have taken that under advisement, but we have no comment to make on the matter yet."

The door to the loft opened, and a breathless Sister Karen rushed in, grocery bags in her arms.

"We just saw you on TV!" Evan cried out excitedly.

"That was taped an hour ago," Karen told them. "What I can't understand is how the media learned about Sanctuary so fast! When I left to go grocery shopping, there were a reporter and a TV camera outside. Now there are three reporters and a whole TV crew! Did any of you guys make phone calls?"

Amy looked around at the residents. No one wore a guilty expression. Then, on TV, one of the news announcers spoke to the other one. "Frank, what do we know about this place Sanctuary?"

"Not much, Sarah. It appears to be some sort of privately funded shelter that takes in children who have been abused or mistreated in some way. Very little is known about the couple in charge, who call themselves Brother James and Sister Karen. Here at *All Day News*, we are attempting to learn more about these people and the situation surrounding little Vikna Doss. Now we turn to examining the progress in the Mideast peace negotiations. . . ."

Sister Karen set the grocery bags down. "I don't advise any of you to go out today, unless you want your face on TV." Amy thought Karen looked very nervous, but she was trying to sound calm for the sake of the kids. "Anyone want to give me a hand putting away the groceries?"

The task had just been completed when the door opened and Brother James came in. Amy thought he'd be upset and angry about the presence of the reporters and TV people outside. Instead, he seemed almost exhilarated. His eyes were bright, practically glowing.

"The networks are out there now," he announced. "They want to know if we've got any sort of official response to that Covalian magistrate. Karen, we need to work up a statement."

Amy was bewildered. "I thought we wanted to avoid publicity for Sanctuary."

"I've changed my mind," James said. "This situation is bigger than anything we've dealt with before. The publicity could work in our favor. We can draw attention to the rights of kids to be where they want to be."

Amy looked at Vikna, still sitting silently in front of the TV. "How do we know Vikna wants to stay here?"

"Wouldn't you rather be in the United States than Covalia?" James asked. "It's a dictatorship, Amy! No one wants to be there, except for the maniacs in power. People are always trying to escape."

"But what about Sanctuary?" Amy asked. "We're not a legal organization. If the authorities know about us, they can close us down!"

"We won't let that happen," James promised her. "And I'll tell you something else. We're going to take advantage of this situation. We're going to give more demonstrations of what Sanctuary is all about. I've got some big plans. Did you know that there's a drug rehabilitation center near here where teenagers can be committed by their parents?"

"But drug addicts *need* rehabilitation," Amy said.

James brushed that aside. "I'll bet you half the kids in residence there don't even touch drugs. Their parents just sent them away to get rid of them. We need to do something for those kids." His voice was becoming more and more excited, and his eyes were flashing.

Karen sat down at the table. "James, I don't want to discuss drug rehab centers at this point. We've got a problem right here and now. I think we should contact the State Department. Perhaps they can arrange a meeting between us and the Covalian representative, so we can discuss what's best for Vikna."

"No!" James declared with such vehemence that even laid-back Max looked startled. "There's nothing to discuss. If we act like we're willing to negotiate, they'll think we're weak. We'll make our statements and that's all."

Karen shook her head. "But if the government gets involved, there's not much we can do, James. We can't fight them!"

James sneered. "They're not so tough."

Now Karen looked alarmed. "James, the secretary of state was on TV! The next thing we know, the President could be involved!"

"Don't be negative!" James yelled. "Haven't you ever heard of David and Goliath?" He stomped out of the room and went upstairs. Karen jumped up from the table and ran after him.

No one had ever heard Brother James yell at Sister Karen like that. Evan was clearly perplexed. "David and Goliath?"

Max explained. "It's a story in the Bible. There was this battle. Goliath was this huge giant, and David was just normal-sized, and David only had a slingshot to fight Goliath. But David won the battle."

Evan was still confused. "Brother James is going to fight the President with a slingshot?"

By now the baby was screaming and some of the other kids had started fighting. There was a knock on the door. At the same time, the phone started ringing.

Only Brother James and Sister Karen could answer doors or phones. The residents all turned to Amy. "What should we do?" Liz asked.

"Don't ask me," Amy said. "I don't know." But of course they would ask her. She was the only adult present. The pounding on the door and the ringing of the phone continued. Amy tried to think like an adult.

"Lisa, take the baby. Liz, go find Sister Karen. Evan, do something with the twins." The ringing and knocking were making Amy nuts. She put her hands over her ears and ran into the kitchen. Max followed her.

"This is getting strange," he said. "Brother James . . . he's acting weird."

"Yeah, I know," Amy said. "I guess he's excited."

"What are we going to do?" Max asked. "What's going to happen?"

He was looking to her for advice and reassurance. She didn't know what to say. How could she tell him that she wasn't really an adult and she knew no more than he did?

Karen flew into the room and grabbed the phone. "Hello? I'm sorry, we have no comment at this time." She hung up the phone. Immediately it began to ring again. She pulled the plug out of the wall. Then she went to the door.

"Who is it?"

"Channel Five, Sister Karen. Can we talk to you?"

"Not now!"

The twins were still squabbling. On the TV screen, the newscaster named Sarah was saying, "We currently have more information about the couple who run Sanctuary, the shelter that is holding Vikna Doss."

"Max, help Evan with the twins," Karen ordered. "Boys, take them upstairs. Now!" They obeyed, and only Amy remained in the room with Karen. They both watched the screen as a picture of Karen appeared.

"It's my yearbook photo, from college," Karen murmured. They listened to the voice of the newscaster.

"Karen Stanton Myers, also known as Sister Karen, has graduate degrees in social work and psychology from Southern State University. Five years ago, she was the plaintiff in the much-publicized Stanton abuse trial, in which she sued her parents for the abuse she suffered as a child. In a verdict that set a precedent, she was awarded one million dollars. At that time, she said she would use the money to help young people in abusive situations."

So that was what paid for Sanctuary, Amy thought.

"Her husband, James Myers, also comes from a troubled background. According to a cousin, he was an extremely intelligent but emotionally unstable child whose parents committed him to a hospital for disturbed teenagers when he was thirteen."

Amy gasped. So that was why James had sympathized with her own escape from a hospital.

"Together, James and Karen Myers established Sanctuary as a private institution that would not have to answer to any official welfare department. The place occasionally operates outside the parameters of the law. There have been stories of young people being taken without permission from homes in which abuse was not proven."

"What sort of proof do you want?" James was at the foot of the stairs, and he was yelling at the TV image. "You want to see some black-and-blue marks? How about a scar or two?"

"This is Sanctuary, a three-floor loft on a street off Sunset Boulevard," the announcer said as the entrance to Sanctuary appeared on the screen.

"Ohmigod," Karen murmured. "Look at all those reporters." There now appeared to be about fifty media people in front of their building.

Amy moved closer to the TV and scrutinized the screen. A figure with a large nose and a sunken chin caught her eye. "That man isn't a reporter! Remember the guy I told you about, the one in the raincoat who's been lurking around? That's him!"

James joined her at the TV. "He could be from the government. They might have sent him to watch us."

"No," Amy said, "I saw him around before Sister Karen brought Vikna here."

"That doesn't mean anything," James snapped. "Maybe the government has been watching us for years."

Karen looked at him in alarm. "James, that's not possible. You're talking nonsense."

But James didn't respond. "I'll go down and give our statement," he said, and went out the door.

A moment later Amy watched him on TV, telling the media that Sanctuary would never relinquish Vikna Doss to the Covalian government—or any other government, for that matter.

From upstairs, Liz yelled, "Sister Karen, the baby won't stop screaming! And one of the twins just threw up!"

Karen put a hand to her head. Amy looked at her sympathetically. "We need help," Amy said.

Karen nodded. "I wish we had another older kid here right now. Someone we could count on, who could understand how the kids here feel."

"I know someone who could help," Amy said suddenly. Someone who could understand young people who had been pushed around. She'd never actually been abused, but she was probably feeling pretty rebellious right about now. And Amy knew that Tasha would be very happy to leave the place where she was currently residing.

She went to the phone and dialed Information. "Could I have the number of Camp Riverbend, please?"

# twelve
## 12

"The executive magistrate of the nation of Covalia has issued a statement demanding that the United States government take appropriate action to secure the release of Vikna Doss from the Sanctuary shelter. What began as the simple rescue of a lost child by Karen Myers is now threatening to become an international incident. The U.S. government has not yet responded to the Covalian demands."

The central figure in the international incident was now sitting at the dining table eating a bowl of cereal, along with the twins. The others watched the all-news station on TV. The television had been on for days now, and barely half an hour passed without some comment about Sanctuary.

"I'll put dinner on the table," Sister Karen said. "There's not much left, though. I haven't been able to get past those reporters to go to the supermarket." At least there were fewer people eating at Sanctuary. The three older boys had left. They'd been asked once too often to help with the baby and the twins, and they'd decided they were better off on the streets. Now Robbie was talking about taking off too.

"Amy," Karen said. "Try to get James to come downstairs and eat something. He won't listen to me."

Amy went upstairs. James sat at the desk in the bedroom, writing feverishly. He'd been up there for hours.

"Aren't you hungry?" Amy asked. "Wouldn't you like something to eat?"

James didn't answer.

"Brother James?"

He looked up. Those dark eyes that had always burned now seemed to be blazing. "Listen to this. 'The world must learn that the sanctity of childhood cannot be violated, not by a parent, not by a government. It is our mission to save children not only from abuse but from potential abuse as well, to provide every child with a nurturing environment in which they are free to make their own decisions as to their welfare.' How does that sound?"

Amy hesitated. "I'm not sure I completely understand it." But James had lost interest in her opinion and was writing again. It was also apparent that he had no interest in food.

Amy went back downstairs. One of the twins had emptied his bowl of cereal on the floor, and Liz was cleaning it up. Lisa was feeding the baby. Amy found Karen in the kitchen, washing dishes and looking absolutely exhausted.

"He's not hungry," Amy reported.

Karen brushed the hair out of her eyes. "Have you been able to reach your friend?"

Amy shook her head. "I'll keep trying." She went back to the phone and dialed. But once again, the camp refused to bring Tasha to the phone. It seemed that only parents were allowed to call the campers. Camp Riverbend seemed to be a prison, just like the hospital Amy had been in, just like the home Evan, the twins, and the baby had come from.

Now Amy was even beginning to feel like she was in another jail here at Sanctuary. She didn't dare go out and risk getting videotaped or photographed by the mob of reporters who were still hanging out in front of their building.

She had to tell Karen she wasn't able to reach her friend. "I know exactly where she is," Amy complained. "It's a camp up north. But she's not allowed to use the phone."

Karen was surprised. "What kind of camp doesn't allow counselors to use the phone?"

Amy realized that Karen thought Tasha had to be an adult, like Amy. "Well, actually she's a camper. But she's thirteen and very reliable. She'd be good with the twins. And I know she doesn't want to be at camp. Her parents forced her to go."

She knew that comment would grab Karen's sympathy. "How far away is the camp?"

"It's about ninety miles north of here."

"Do you want to go get her?"

Amy looked at Karen blankly. "How could I do that?"

"You could take my car."

Now Amy was confused. "You have a car? Then why didn't Brother James use it to rescue Evan and the others?"

"He takes medication, so he's not supposed to drive. And the car is registered to me. If he were to be caught behind the wheel, we could both be arrested, and we can't let that happen. For the sake of Sanctuary."

"He takes medication for what?"

Sister Karen seemed reluctant to answer, and Amy waited. Finally Karen said, "It's a chemical thing, in his brain. It's hard for him to control his temper. That's why his parents put him in that hospital years ago. It was totally unnecessary for him to be hospitalized. He's fine as long as he takes the pills. But the pills affect his vision, so he can't have a driver's license."

So it was better for James to "borrow" a stranger's car than to take his own wife's. It was weird, but Amy supposed it made sense. Thinking about James's problem with his temper made her wonder if he'd been taking all his pills lately. The realization that she had been a passenger in a "borrowed" car with a mentally unstable driver gave her the creeps. And now here she was, about to borrow a car herself, with no license to drive it.

Taking her cue from the stranger who had been lurking outside, she put on a hooded raincoat and pulled the drawstring tight so the folds of the hood completely covered her face. If her photo was taken, and even if it appeared on TV or in a newspaper, her mother wouldn't recognize her. She would leave at three o'clock in the morning. If the reporters followed their routine of the past few days, they would have gone away by then anyway.

But there were still a couple of people hanging out

in front of Sanctuary. Clutching the keys to Sister Karen's car tightly, Amy ran out of the building at top speed.

She was aware of the astonished expression on the face of the reporter she passed. The other person was the mysterious man in the raincoat. He didn't look as astonished—in fact, Amy could have sworn that she saw the glimmer of a smile on his face. But she couldn't waste time thinking about that now. She had to find the car, and then she had to find Camp Riverbend.

The car was easy enough to locate—it was right where Karen had told her it would be. Luckily, it was pretty similar to the car that Amy's mother owned, and Amy had certainly watched her mother drive many times. From memory, she was able to get the car started and out of the parking lot. She stopped at a gas station to fill up the tank and buy a map. Within minutes she was on the freeway, heading north.

At this time of night, there wasn't too much traffic, which was a relief. While Amy could drive the car, she couldn't say she felt very comfortable. Every time she passed another car, she wondered if the driver had any idea that a thirteen-year-old was behind the wheel.

Glancing at herself in the rearview mirror, she knew that wasn't likely. She also knew it wasn't going to be easy convincing Tasha that she was Amy Candler. As she was considering how best to approach her friend, she became aware of a bright light just behind her car. She looked into the mirror. It was a police car, and it was following her closely. The light was flashing. Then the siren came on.

Now what? Step hard on the gas pedal and try to get away? She knew from watching car chases on cop "reality" shows that the police always caught up to the bad guy. How strange to realize that *she* was a bad guy—an underage runaway posing as an adult, driving a car without a license. Would she be treated like a child or an adult? Would they put her in jail or call her mother? She wasn't sure which would be worse.

The police were making their move. They were coming around to the side of her car. Once the officer could see her, he'd order her to get off the freeway. She wondered if he'd be pointing a gun.

The car pulled alongside her . . . and kept on going. Its speed increased, and soon it was just a speck in the distance. It was after somebody else.

The rest of the trip was uneventful. Amy located the correct exit and drove the car off the freeway. She was in the country now, and she rolled down the windows to get some fresh air. She needed the air to wake herself up. It was now almost five in the morning. She considered pulling the car over to the side of the road and taking a quick nap, but she was so close now. Besides, it would probably be a lot easier to get Tasha out of the camp at this hour than in broad daylight with everyone awake.

Spotting a sign that read WELCOME TO CAMP RIVER-BEND, she turned onto the dirt road. After a moment the road divided, and there were two signs. One pointed to the right and read GIRLS' CAMP. The boys' camp was on the left.

Amy turned to the right and started down the narrow path. But she didn't get very far. All the campers and their counselors might have been sound asleep at five in the morning, but the uniformed guards at the security station weren't. And they didn't exactly welcome her to Camp Riverbend.

Three of them, big guys, gathered around her car. If she tried to make a run for it, she'd hit at least one of them. And she wasn't about to add murder to the list of crimes she'd already committed.

"Could I see some identification, please?"

Amy offered a weak smile. "I don't have any."

"What's your business here?"

"I just came to visit someone."

"At five o'clock in the morning?"

She couldn't think of an answer. At least nothing

that would satisfy these guys. So without another word, she shifted into reverse and backed out onto the main road.

But she hadn't come this far to go back to Sanctuary without bringing some help. Somewhere on the other side of the camp, Eric was sleeping. Maybe he could think of a way to get to Tasha.

This time Amy didn't try to get the car past any security station. She parked it on the side of the road. When she got out, she saw the guards up ahead. But before they could see her, she ducked behind some bushes and began crawling. She figured that if she got caught, she could always pretend she was a counselor from the girls' side who'd lost her way in the darkness.

As it turned out, she had nothing to worry about. The guards on the boys' side weren't quite as diligent as the ones on the girls'. They were talking as she crept silently by the station, and no one noticed her.

But now she had to find Eric, and she had no idea what cabin he was in. She started with the first one, grabbing the ledge of a window so she could peer inside. There were six beds, three against each wall, and each held a young boy.

A door that was slightly ajar seemed to lead to a second room—maybe that was where the counselors slept, she thought. At the other end of the cabin was an open alcove, and she caught a glimpse of a bed in there, too. She figured the private room was for the real counselor, and the junior counselor slept in the alcove.

She strained to get a look at the figure lying in the alcove bed. She stretched herself as far as possible, and then—she lost her grip and fell to the ground with a thud that was very loud in the silence.

She could hear a cry from inside, and then footsteps coming from the alcove. She held her breath and put her ear against the wall so she could listen.

The voice of a small boy said, "I heard something! Outside!"

"There's no one outside. It was a frog or something like that," answered the voice of an older boy—but it wasn't Eric.

The little boy wasn't convinced. "It would have to be an awfully big frog to make that kind of noise!"

The junior counselor was coming toward the window. Amy pressed herself even closer against the wall.

"Well, the giant frog's taken off. Go back to sleep."

When all was quiet, Amy moved on to the next cabin. Now that she knew where the junior counselors slept, she went directly to the window at that end of the cabin. In this cabin, the boy slept facedown with the sheet over his head, but unless Eric had gained an awful lot of weight at camp, it couldn't be him. It felt weird, spying on strange sleeping boys.

She spotted Eric in the fourth cabin she checked. Now she had to figure out how to make him spot her without alerting the others. Eric was a notoriously sound sleeper. Sometimes it took three alarm clocks, his mother, *and* his sister to get him awake in the morning. Amy figured it would be even harder at this hour.

The window was open, and she scratched at the screen. "Eric," she whispered. Then, a little more loudly, "Eric!"

One of the boys in the center room stirred. But the figure in the junior counselor's bed didn't. Carefully Amy tried to lift the screen and prayed it wouldn't squeak. It did—and now two campers shifted around in their beds. But Eric didn't budge.

Amy debated her next move. It was too bad she didn't have a griddle and pancake batter handy. Food smells were the one thing that could always get Eric up.

And then, miracle of miracles—just as she had decided to start making loud cricket noises, Eric's eyes opened. He saw the face in the window and sat up, a startled expression on his face. Amy knew he had to be shocked to see a face there, in what he must think was the middle of the night, peering through the window of his cabin.

She beckoned for him to come outside, and he must have recognized her because he leaped out of bed. She watched him tiptoe through the cabin in his bare feet and pajamas. Then he was outside.

He walked toward her in a funny way, like he was swaggering. Then he grinned. "Hiya, pretty lady. Are you lost?"

"No, silly, I came looking for you! I couldn't get into Tasha's camp. I need your help."

His smile wavered. He stared at her with doubt in his eyes and rubbed them as if he wasn't sure what he was seeing.

"Eric?"

"How do you know my name?" he asked uncertainly.

"Eric! Eric, it's me!"

"Who's me?"

She glared at him. "So you call every girl you see 'pretty lady'?"

He gulped and stared at her in disbelief.

"Amy?"

# thirteen
**13**

Eric rubbed his eyes again, harder this time. He had to be dreaming, that was all there was to it. This woman was no ghost, no apparition—she was simply a sleep fantasy. He'd been having some pretty weird dreams lately, mostly nightmarish ones populated with frightening creatures who bore a close resemblance to Steve, the senior counselor. This was the first time in a long while that Eric had been in a normal adolescent dream world with a great-looking woman.

Too bad she wasn't smiling. And would a true teen male fantasy take him by the shoulders and shake him until he could hear his teeth rattle?

"Eric! Look at me! Look in my eyes! It's me, it's Amy!"

What a coincidence, he thought. The supermodel in his dream had the same name as his girlfriend in real life. But would a real supermodel yell like this?

"You want to know why I didn't show up at my own birthday party?" she was saying. "I didn't have an attack of appendicitis. I woke up on my birthday and I looked like this! Something was put inside me when I was cloned, some sort of time-release implant, and it made my cells start developing faster, and when I turned thirteen, I turned into an adult! Overnight!"

The fantasy was talking so fast, he was having a hard time following her. It was sort of annoying that he couldn't control the pace of his own dream.

And the girl wouldn't stop talking. "It's really me, Eric! I can prove it! Remember when we were at Wilderness Adventure and our counselor was murdered? How about the time when we were trapped in the gym at Parkside and almost got crushed between the bleachers? Remember when Jeanine died and everyone thought I killed her? Remember how mad you were when I went to Paris and you found out that I kissed Andy on top of the Eiffel Tower?"

He frowned. "I didn't know you really *kissed* him."

Finally he seemed to be opening his eyes for real, and he gasped loudly. "Wow. It's really you."

"That's what I've been saying, dummy."

He ignored the insult and listened to her story. If it had involved anyone other than Amy, it would have been totally beyond belief. But since his girlfriend's entire life was like something out of science fiction, he had to believe what he heard.

He had known he wasn't being told the truth before. He had been sure she wasn't lying in a hospital recovering from a normal appendectomy. But never in a million years would he have guessed that she'd aged at least ten years overnight. Or that she had run away from the hospital and hid out in a shelter for abused kids. Or that the shelter happened to be the place he'd read about in a newspaper just the day before.

"You're living at Sanctuary? The place where they're hiding the little kid from Covalia? What's her name?"

"Vikna Doss, and we're not *hiding* her," Amy corrected him. "We're protecting her, we're saving her from being sent back to that terrible place. Anyway, we're in a crisis, because we've got other little kids to take care of besides Vikna. We need help. That's why I came here, to get Tasha. She's good with little kids, and I know she'll be absolutely thrilled to get out of here."

"Don't be so sure of that," Eric said.

"What do you mean?"

"I mean, believe it or not, she *likes* this place. She's riding skits and writing horses—no, wait, I mean writing skits and riding horses. And throwing pots, whatever that means. Anyway, she's happy here. *I'm* the one who's miserable."

"Why?"

He filled her in on his crummy experiences at Camp Riverbend and what a disappointment the place had turned out to be. "No one even cares about the campers. Half of them were dumped here by parents who just don't want to have them around."

"Oh, I know exactly what you mean," Amy said fervently. "I used to think my mother could be a real pain. But when I heard what's happened to some of the Sanctuary kids . . ." She shook her head wearily. "It's horrible, how any adult can be so cruel to a child."

"Especially a parent," Eric added. He gazed at Amy in wonderment. Funny how he was able to talk to her like she was still the girl who lived next door to him. He could feel himself blushing. This was an older woman, a grown-up lady! "Geez, do you realize, you're old enough to be a mother now?" he blurted out.

Now it was Amy's turn to go pink. "Yeah, well, maybe I look like someone who could be a mother, but that's all just physical stuff. Inside, I'm still me and I'm only thirteen. And I'm definitely not ready to have any babies. Not yet."

That cheered him up. "So, maybe you could wait until I'm old enough too?"

She gave him a funny little crooked grin, and for a second she almost looked like the Amy he knew. "Yeah, I might." She was beet red now, and she turned away to look in the direction of the girls' camp.

"So you don't think Tasha will want to go back to Sanctuary with me?"

"Oh, I guess she'd go if you asked her," he replied.

"But she likes being here at camp."

"Yeah." After a second he added, "Amy . . . *I* know how to change diapers too."

She blinked, like the idea was a total revelation to her.

Suddenly the main door of the cabin flew open. The Creature from the Black Lagoon, otherwise known as Steve, the senior counselor, stood there, and he looked meaner than usual.

"What's going on, Morgan?" he barked. "What are you doing out here?" Then he saw that Eric wasn't alone, and his eyes widened. His expression and his tone of voice changed dramatically.

"Wow, where'd you find the fabulous *babe*?" He

focused his attention on Amy. "Hey, sweetie, what are you doing with a little boy like that? Wouldn't you rather be with a real man?"

"Sure," Amy replied sweetly. "And if you know a real man, I'd be happy to meet him. Otherwise, I think I'll stick with Eric."

Steve glared at her. "I'm calling Security. Chicks aren't allowed on this side of the lake. Morgan, get inside."

Eric glared right back at him. "Drop dead." It wasn't a very original expression, but the message was clear. The fabulous babe grabbed his hand, and together they ran off.

# fourteen

**A** t about noon Amy was turning off the freeway she'd entered nine hours earlier. It had taken them longer to get back to L.A. than she'd thought it would, mainly because Eric refused to appear at Sanctuary—or anywhere else—dressed in pajamas. So they'd had to wait till they could find an open store that sold guys' clothes.

But then there was the fact that neither of them had any money. They lucked out, though. The man in the clothing store wasn't going to offer them anything for free, but he directed them to a local homeless shelter that gave away food and used clothing.

Eric had been kind of quiet ever since. Stopping at a traffic light, Amy glanced at him. "You don't look so bad," she assured him. The pajama top could pass as a regular shirt. The faded purple jogging pants were worn at the knees and too short for him, and the beat-up tennis shoes had a lot of holes, but at least he didn't look like someone who had just gotten out of bed.

Eric was no longer concerned about the way he looked, though. "You know, Amy, there were people at that shelter who weren't any older than I am."

"I know," Amy said. "It makes you think. We've been pretty lucky."

"I'm never going to complain about my home and my family again," Eric declared.

"Me neither," Amy agreed.

"*You've* got nothing to complain about," Eric pointed out. "You're an adult—you can do anything you want."

"But what if I want to be thirteen years old?" she asked.

He had no answer for that.

They were stuck in typical Los Angeles traffic, and Amy turned on the radio. She fiddled with the dial, searching for an all-news station that might give a traffic report. She finally got the report—which only confirmed that there was no way to avoid traffic jams in

L.A. But the news that came after the report was more interesting.

"As we reported to you at nine o'clock this morning, the Supreme Court has determined that little Vikna Doss, the sole survivor of that tragedy on a supply ship, must be returned to the custody of her family in Covalia. The Sanctuary shelter was ordered to bring the child to an undisclosed Los Angeles location before noon today, to turn her over to Covalian officials. As of noon, no representative from Sanctuary has appeared at the designated meeting place. Sanctuary is being held in contempt of court, and we await a decision from the courts as to what the next step will be."

Amy sucked in her breath and searched for a way out of the traffic jam. Eventually the traffic began to move again, and within half an hour she was pulling into the same parking space she'd vacated at three that morning. Moments later she and Eric were approaching Sanctuary.

They had to push and shove just to get onto the side street that led to the entrance. There were about three times as many reporters and camera crews as before, plus police, plus demonstrators carrying signs that demanded FREE VIKNA DOSS. Amy didn't know whether the demonstrators wanted Sanctuary to free the child or wanted her to be free to stay in the United States, and it didn't really matter to her. All she wanted was to get herself and Eric inside the building.

Finally they reached the door. Max must have been watching through the peephole, because as soon as they were there the door opened a crack. Amy slipped in, but Max tried to close the door on Eric.

"No, Max, it's okay—this is my friend Eric. He's come to help us. He knows about our situation."

Max let him in and asked, "You know about drugs, Eric?"

Eric was taken aback. "No thanks, man! I'm an athlete, I don't touch the stuff."

Max rolled his eyes. "I'm not offering. I was just hoping you might know what to do with drug addicts."

"What are you talking about?" Amy asked.

Max explained. Brother James had acted on his idea of the day before. He'd broken into a drug rehabilitation hospital and liberated two teenagers. "But I'm thinking maybe they were better off in the hospital. 'Cause they're not doing too well here."

He wasn't the only one who thought so. In the kitchen Amy found Sister Karen arguing with Brother James.

"We can't help them here!" she was saying. "They're going through withdrawal. They need professional medical care. They're sick, James!"

"It was the hospital that made them sick," James declared angrily. "They pump these kids full of chemicals so the kids believe they're addicted!"

Amy tried to break into the conversation. "Sister Karen, Brother James, this is my friend—" She froze when Brother James turned and looked at her wildly.

"You know what I'm talking about, Amy! You were in a hospital. They put stuff into you, didn't they? Just like they did to me!"

"I—I don't know," she began hesitantly.

He turned to Eric. "It's a conspiracy, you realize that, don't you? And there are an awful lot of people who are in on it, people you'd never suspect. The guy who rings up your groceries in the supermarket. The guy who bags them. He could be one of them."

Eric was clearly bewildered. "I'm sorry, I don't know what you're talking about."

Behind Brother James, Sister Karen had begun to cry. Brother James ignored her and continued to address Eric. "Did you see all those reporters out there? They're not all reporters, you know. Some of them are spies."

"Spies," Amy repeated. "From . . . from the government?"

James shook his head. "You saw one of them, Amy, remember? The one in the raincoat, with the big nose?

**139**

He's been there long before the reporters, watching us, waiting for his chance."

"His chance for what?" Eric asked, but James kept his eyes on Amy.

"We're talking about something bigger here, Amy. Something beyond our government, beyond our world!"

Eric tried to smile. "You mean, like, spies from another planet?"

Now he had James's attention. "Don't joke!" James cried out. "This is serious!"

He began pacing the kitchen and mumbling to himself. Amy turned to Karen, who still had her hands over her face. "Where are the others? Where's Vikna?"

Karen took her hands from her face and spoke through her tears. "Upstairs. I told all of them to stay upstairs." She looked at James, who was still pacing and mumbling. "He's sick, Amy. Very sick. He stopped taking his medications."

From upstairs there came a howling sound. "That's one of the boys James brought back from the hospital," Karen told them. "I'd better go see him. Eric, could you help me?"

Eric looked at Amy, who nodded. "I'm okay, you go on and help Karen."

With one last worried look at James, Karen hurried out of the kitchen, and Eric followed her.

Amy spoke softly. "Brother James? Don't you think you should take your pills?"

"Pills," James muttered. "Pills, pills, pills. That's part of the plan, you know. They want to medicate us, tranquilize us, turn us into happy robots so we won't have any passion, so we won't fight. That's why they can get away with hurting children. No one argues, no one fights for the kids. Well, *I'm* not going to stop fighting. And now I've got a weapon."

Amy could feel her heart begin to beat faster. She tried to keep her voice calm. "What kind of weapon do you have, Brother James?"

He reached into a paper bag that was lying on the counter and pulled out something long and metallic. It didn't look like a gun or a bomb, but Amy stepped back warily. "What is that?" It looked oddly familiar—and then she recognized it. Dr. Dave had shown her one in his office. "It's a laser, isn't it? It uses some sort of electronic beams, so people don't always have to be cut open in operations."

Brother James beamed at her. "Very good! But a laser can do other things too. It all depends on what you're aiming at. And how strong the beam is."

Amy eyed the thing apprehensively. She wasn't sure it could do any real damage to anyone, but she didn't want to find out.

There was a knock on the door. Amy went to it and peered out the peephole. She recognized the big nose and small chin immediately.

James was just behind her. "Who is it?"

"It's . . . um, it's one of the people from downstairs, I guess he was able to get past Max. Don't worry, I won't let him in."

"Let him in, let him in!" Brother James cried out. "I'd like to see a reporter right now. I want to tell him what I know about the worldwide conspiracy. Then he could go on TV and tell the world!"

He pushed Amy aside and jerked open the door. Then he stepped back, and his skin turned ashen. *"You."*

The man in the raincoat walked in calmly, and he didn't even look at Brother James. "Hello, Amy. I think you should come with me."

To her eyes, the man looked much scarier than the laser. He must have scared Brother James, too, because James turned and ran back to the kitchen. The man didn't seem to care; he only had eyes for Amy. And he was smiling, a horrible smile that gave her chills. "It's time, Amy. You know that, don't you?"

Amy could hear how unsteady her voice was. "Who are you? How do you know my name?"

She didn't know whether he would answer her, and

she would never have a chance to find out. A high-pitched whine filled the air, and a streak of white light shot past her. The man in the raincoat had no time to react, not even to change his expression. He continued to smile as he fell to the ground, and he was smiling as he lay there, very still. And very dead.

From the staircase came a shriek. Evan was there, along with Lisa and Liz, and they were all looking at Brother James in horror. Sister Karen came down behind them, with Vikna in her arms, and Eric followed.

Sister Karen's eyes darted back and forth between her husband and the man on the floor. Then there was a louder sound that came from outside.

Someone was speaking through a bullhorn. "This is the chief of a government battalion speaking. We have been ordered to remove the child Vikna Doss from Sanctuary by any means necessary, including force. You have ten minutes to bring the child outside."

Brother James laughed savagely. "Just let them try, let them try!" He aimed his laser gun at the door.

"No, James." Sister Karen came down the stairs. "It's over. If they storm this place, people will get hurt. Our other residents will be in danger. Everyone, go back up to the bedroom."

The residents obeyed. Only Eric remained on the stairs, watching the scene as if he couldn't quite believe it was a reality. Amy was having a hard time believing it herself.

But she wasn't frightened, just overwhelmingly sad. She didn't want to shriek; she wanted to cry. She looked at Brother James and remembered when his passion had been directed toward real and important goals. Now, without his medication, the passion was no longer focused on anything real. His poor troubled mind had sent him over the edge.

"I'm bringing Vikna out to the authorities," Sister Karen said quietly.

"No," Brother James answered. "No, you're not. I can't let you do this. She's better off dead than going back to Covalia." He raised the laser and pointed it.

Karen froze. But Amy didn't. As that horrible high-pitched whine filled the air, she moved faster than the speed of light, intercepting the white beam before it could hit Vikna or Karen. Her body was filled with a painless warmth.

And then—nothing.

# f i f t e e n

From the staircase, Eric watched in horror as Amy fell to the floor. In that second, the room was like a freeze-frame from a video—no one moved, and there was utter silence. Then the door to the loft opened and a frantic Max stood there.

"Brother James, they're coming! The military guys! And I can't stop them!"

His announcement distracted Brother James just long enough for Eric to leap over the staircase rail and come crashing down on him. The laser was knocked out of James's hands. Then came the sound of pounding feet as the government's rescue squad came tearing up the stairs.

Screams of panic filled the air. There was utter chaos, but Eric couldn't let that stop him. He had a mission. Rushing to Amy, he picked her up in his arms and headed resolutely toward the exit. In the commotion and confusion of the scene, he walked right out the door.

He had no idea whether she was alive or dead, and he couldn't take the time to feel for a pulse. He had to get her out of there, away from that crazy Brother James, away from these hyper raiders. It didn't matter whether the rescue squad was military, government, police, whatever. Amy was in as much danger from authorities as she was from any laser-bearing lunatic.

A curious crowd, drawn by the noise and the TV cameras, had gathered around the building. Eric lowered Amy, letting her feet drag on the ground while keeping a firm grip around her waist and resting her head on his shoulder. He hoped that anyone who saw them would think they were just a loving couple. He got them both through the crowd, down the street, and into the lot where they'd left Sister Karen's car.

Thank goodness the keys were still in Amy's pocket. He arranged her in the front passenger's seat and took his place behind the wheel. The car wasn't difficult to start up, but even after the motor had been humming steadily for a minute, he remained still.

He'd never driven a car before. This fall, in high

school, he would start taking driver's education, but he had never been in control of a vehicle. When he was a little kid his father had let him sit on his lap once in a while and pretend he was steering. But that was about it.

Still, he'd watched people drive, and it didn't look that hard. He knew which pedal was the gas and which one was the brake, so he thought he'd be okay. He shifted into reverse and applied pressure on the accelerator.

But the car wasn't in reverse, and he was putting too much pressure on the pedal. The car leaped forward. He slammed on the brake just fast enough to avoid hitting another parked car. Somehow, after two more attempts, he managed to get the car out onto the street, but that was where his troubles really began.

The cars on the road weren't parked and standing still—they were moving around him, in front of him, behind him, and beside him. He struggled to keep the car going at the same pace in a straight line, and despite the way the car shuddered and inched along, he thought he was doing okay. But he caught glimpses of other drivers eyeing him suspiciously and nervously.

He tried to turn, but he must have jerked the wheel too far over, because he practically hit another car coming from the opposite direction. The other car swerved to avoid him, and the driver hit the horn furiously.

Other cars began doing the same, and in his rearview mirror, Eric could see that the noise had attracted the attention of a police officer on a motorcycle. In a minute, he knew, the cop would be after him.

He managed to get around another corner, turned the car into a driveway, and slammed on the brakes so hard he almost hit the windshield. But the car stopped, and he turned off the engine. Moving rapidly, he crawled over the back of his seat, and from that position he pushed Amy into the seat behind the wheel. Then he crawled over into the passenger seat.

He was still trying to catch his breath when the motorcycle pulled up beside him. The police officer got off his bike and approached the driver's side of the car. He was speaking before he got a look inside. "Would you please get out of the car, ma'am?"

Eric leaned over her and spoke anxiously. "Officer, she passed out! I don't know what's wrong with her, I don't even know if she's alive! I was trying to steer the car from over here!"

The police officer frowned. He placed two fingers on Amy's neck, feeling for a pulse. Then he jerked his hand back as if he'd been burned. "It's going wild," he said in alarm, and got on his radio. Moments later Eric heard an approaching ambulance.

As the men gently lifted Amy onto a stretcher, Eric

told the ambulance driver to take her to a particular hospital. It was the one where Dr. Hopkins worked, and Eric hoped Dr. Dave could get to Amy before anyone else started fooling around with tests and other medical procedures.

"Can I come with you?" Eric asked the ambulance attendants.

"Sure," one of them said kindly. "Do you want to ride in the back with your mother?"

Aghast, Eric felt his mouth fall open. But he didn't think this was the appropriate moment to clear up his relationship with the patient. "Yeah, okay." And he climbed into the back with the stretcher.

# sixteen 16

It was like coming inside from heavy, cold fog and finding yourself in a cozy, warm, comfortable home. It didn't matter that the home was all white and smelled like antiseptic, or that there was a tube in her nose and another running into her arm. Maybe it was her mother's face that made it seem so inviting.

Nancy Candler's eyes were surrounded by dark circles, and anxiety lines crisscrossed her forehead. But she was smiling. "Welcome back, sweetie," she said.

"Hi, Mom," Amy murmured, her voice sounding thick and unnatural to her own ears. "Where am I?"

"Back in the hospital. I'm afraid we couldn't get you

back into that nice room, though. Some movie star needs it for her tummy tuck."

"That's okay. How long have I been here?"

"Just over twenty-four hours. You're going to be okay." Nancy reached down and pushed a lock of hair away from Amy's face.

"Mom?"

"Yes?"

"I'm sorry I had to run away like that. I didn't want to make you worry. But no one would listen to me—not you, not Dr. Dave. I had to do what I thought was best for me."

"I know, dear."

"And, Mom, once I'm feeling okay, I want to leave the hospital. I don't want any more tests or X rays. I want to go home. I have to find a normal life for myself. I'm an adult now, Mom. You have to listen to me."

"I know," her mother said again. "And I will." She bent down and kissed Amy's forehead. It was soothing, and Amy felt herself drifting off to sleep.

When she woke up later on, she was alone in the room. The first thing she was aware of was the absence of those tubes. The next thing she realized was that her head was clear. She felt fine.

Still, she eased herself cautiously out of the bed and

planted her feet firmly on the floor before she tried to stand. She felt a little strange—not bad, just different. She rose and made her way carefully to the bathroom. Running some cold water into the sink, she splashed her face, and as she did so, she caught sight of her reflection in the mirror.

For a moment she just stared at the face with the water trickling down her cheeks and nose. She knew that face. But it wasn't the face she'd seen the day before.

Dr. Dave appeared in the mirror. She turned to him. He smiled.

"It was the laser," he told her. "Pure luck, I suppose. The beam hit the implant and dissolved it. And overnight, you became . . ."

"Twelve again," Amy breathed. "No! Thirteen. Wow, I almost forgot."

"You check out perfectly normal," Dr. Dave said. "Well, as normal as you ever were. And you can go home soon."

"Today?"

"Well, I'd rather you wait until tomorrow. If it's okay with you," he added hastily.

Amy considered this. "I guess I can handle one more day here." She was about to ask him to tell her what had happened to Eric and everyone else when a voice came over a speaker.

"Dr. Hopkins, please report to the emergency room."

"I've gotta run," Dr. Dave said. "I'll stop by to see you later."

For a while Amy remained in the bathroom, studying herself in the mirror. There she was, just as she used to be. Five feet tall, about a hundred pounds. Plain brown eyes, straight brown hair. A figure that didn't look any different at the age of the thirteen than it had looked when she was twelve.

With a sigh, she went back into the room, sat down on the bed, and picked up the TV remote.

". . . And so, once again, peace negotiations in the Mideast have broken down. Now, on to local news. In the aftermath of the Sanctuary raid, the military and the police have been praised by the mayor for their handling of the crisis. None of the young residents were injured in the raid, and little Vikna Doss has been safely delivered to her family in Covalia. A local TV station witnessed their reunion."

On the screen Amy saw a little girl whose resemblance to the child she'd known at Sanctuary was limited to size and coloring. The big difference was in her expression—she was smiling and laughing with a happy-looking group of people who were clearly well known to her. Brother James had been wrong. She wouldn't have been better off dead.

"The death of James Myers, also known as Brother James, has been ruled a suicide. Apparently, the co-director of Sanctuary turned the laser that was stolen from Western Rehabilitation Clinic on himself. There has been no sign of the other director, Karen Stanton Myers. Police would like to question her.

"In a follow-up to our earlier report, we now know that the teenagers with drug dependency problems who were found at Sanctuary during the raid have been returned to Western Rehab. All the other young people have been placed in appropriate residential care. We spoke with one of them this afternoon."

It was Max. He still looked pale and shaken, but when he spoke to the reporter, his voice was calm. "Brother James was a good person," he said. "He wasn't evil, and he didn't want to hurt anyone. He believed in saving children, and he just got carried away by what he believed in. When he stopped taking his pills, he just couldn't control his feelings anymore."

The reporter asked Max about his own situation now, and Max spoke cautiously. "I'm staying with some nice people. I don't know how long it will last, though. I'm kind of used to being on my own."

"Do you still think of Sanctuary as your home?"

"Yeah, kind of. And I miss the people. I guess I'll still be able to see most of them, but some just vanished. Like Amy, this woman who worked there. I don't know what happened to her. I'd like to see her again."

But he wouldn't, not in any way that would make sense to him. Amy's eyes filled with tears.

The tears were hastily wiped away when her door opened. Eric was carrying a birthday cake with thirteen blazing candles. After he had sung "Happy Birthday to You" and she had blown out the candles, he set the cake down and embraced her.

"Tasha will be so bummed she missed all the excitement!" he said.

Amy laughed. "She'll have to wait awhile to see what I look like as a grown-up."

"Yeah, I should have taken a picture," Eric said. He sat down on the bed. "It's nice to have you back the way you were."

"Really?" Amy asked anxiously. "But you thought I was a babe!"

"Yeah," Eric admitted. "But I think we go together better like this."

A moment later a nurse came in and shooed him out, saying Amy needed her rest. Amy felt absolutely fine, but within fifteen minutes of Eric's departure, she fell asleep again.

When she woke the room was dark. She turned to the window and saw that it was nighttime. It had to be pretty late, and she was still sleepy. She wasn't sure what had woken her . . . until she realized she wasn't alone in the room.

A figure stood in the shadow near the door. It didn't take Amy long to recognize Sister Karen. Amy sat up in bed, suddenly wide awake.

"I hope I didn't frighten you," Karen whispered.

"No, it's okay. I wondered what happened to you." Amy patted the side of her bed. Karen walked over and sat down. Amy drew the bedspread up to her nose, but it wasn't really necessary to hide herself. The room was nearly pitch black, and Karen was wearing sunglasses.

"I can only stay a minute," Karen said. "I have to get away. The police are looking for me."

"But you didn't do anything wrong," Amy protested. "They can't arrest you, can they?"

Karen smiled sadly. "I don't want to find out—that's why I'm leaving town. But I had to come to you first. There was something I wanted you to see."

She opened her bag and rummaged through it. "The man James killed, the one in the raincoat . . . I saw something fall out of his pocket when he fell. I picked it up." She unfolded the paper and held it toward Amy. "It's you, isn't it?"

It wasn't an ordinary photograph or drawing. It looked like a computer printout. Amy recalled seeing something like it on a missing persons poster in the post office: a computer-generated projection of what a person would probably look like after a certain number of years. That was what this was—last year's school photo of Amy, digitally manipulated to add ten years to her age.

There were no other identifying marks on the paper— at least, she didn't see anything right away. But then her unusually keen vision picked something up—a watermark in the corner. In the shape of a crescent moon.

"I don't know what it means," Karen said, "but I thought you should have it." She cocked her head to one side. "You seem—different. Are you all right?"

"Yes, I'm fine now."

Karen leaned forward and kissed Amy's cheek. "Goodbye, Amy. Thank you." And then she was gone.

Alone now, Amy examined the picture more closely. The manipulation was well done. No wonder the man had been able to recognize her.

And Amy knew he was from the organization. He was one of the Project Crescent people. They were still after her. They must have known about the implant, that this rapid aging process would happen to her, and they had wanted her. Would they still want her, now that she was a kid again? The thought made her shudder. Maybe Brother James had done her a favor by killing this man.

But there would be others.

She looked at the picture again. She'd have to show it to Eric and Tasha, maybe even give them a copy. She had a feeling that Eric would like to have something to remind him of how she had looked.

It could be a souvenir for her, too. She could see what she would look like in the future and remember those days when she'd managed to become an adult slightly ahead of schedule.

Not that she was ever likely to forget.

# Don't miss

# replica

## #17

## Missing Pieces

Something weird is happening to talented students at Parkside Middle School. It's as if someone—or something—is stealing what makes each of them special. And it starts with the jocks.

The star quarterback loses his arm.

The top sprinter becomes slow as molasses.

The basketball team's high scores plummet.

Amy watches all this in bewilderment. Then, as others at school suffer a loss of their talents, Amy decides it's time for action. But she doesn't have a clue what she's up against. . . .